Turtle on a Fence Post

Turtle on a Fence Post

JUNE RAE WOOD

G. P. Putnam's Sons • New York

G. P. Putnam's Sons, a division of The Putnam & Grosset Group,
200 Madison Avenue, New York, NY 10016.
G. P. Putnam's Sons, Reg. U.S. Pat. & Tm. Off.
Published simultaneously in Canada
Printed in the United States of America
Designed by Gunta Alexander. Text set in Bembo

Library of Congress Cataloging-in-Publication Data
Wood, June Rae. Turtle on a fence post / June Rae Wood.
p. cm. Summary: A grumpy old veteran with his own history
of grief helps fourteen-year-old Delrita release the pent-up emotions
she holds following the death of her parents.
[1. Grief—Fiction. 2. Guilt—Fiction. 3. Emotions—Fiction.]
I. Title. PZ7.W84965Tu 1997 [Fic]—dc21 96-53622 CIP AC
ISBN 0-399-23184-6 10 9 8 7 6 5 4 3 2 1 First Impression

I am grateful to the veterans of World War II who shared their stories with me during the eight years I worked for a newspaper. Facts reported by these men helped me to create the fictional character Orvis Roebuck.

This book is dedicated to all veterans who saw the shadow of death as they fought for freedom. They are the true American heroes.

Contents

1

A Woman
Possessed

"Well, I declare," said Aunt Queenie. "That father of mine's left the lid off the sugar bowl, and now ants are invading my kitchen!"

I glanced up from my woodcarving project and saw her jabbing furiously at black dots on the counter.

"Death to you!" she cried. "And you . . . and you . . . and you!"

Her hand was a blur of wristwatch and lavender nail polish, and I couldn't help but grin. This must be the first army in history to be wiped out with one finger.

"Delrita Jensen," she said, frowning at me over her shoulder, "it's not funny. These insects could carry any number of diseases. We don't know where they've been."

"Sorry." I ducked my head, letting my long brown hair hide the smile that I couldn't wipe off my face. Aunt Queenie was a germ warrior, and the whole house was her battleground. Peeking out from beneath the hair, I watched as she waged war against the dots.

Her necklace and earrings lay in a shiny purple heap on the counter, and she'd tied an apron around her waist. Other than that, she was still dolled up in the outfit she'd worn for her volunteer shift at the crisis center—a royal purple dress with matching high-heeled shoes. Her straw-colored hair was tortured into a topknot, which sat like a bird's nest on her head. From the nest protruded her trademark—a pencil. Today's pencil was purple to match her outfit.

After wetting a sponge at the sink, she went back to the ants. "I don't know why that man can't remember to put a lid on a sugar bowl," she said, raking the sponge across the counter to gather up the bodies in one fell swoop.

I kept an eye on her as she cleaned behind the canister set and straightened each piece so the flower motifs faced front. Aunt Queenie's world would stop spinning if those flowers weren't in perfect alignment. "The coffee is a smidgen off-center," I said with a straight face.

She moved the coffee can a fraction of an inch. "Is that better?"

"Now the tea."

She adjusted the tea can.

"Now turn the coffee a teensy bit to the left."

"That's back where I started," she said, turning the coffee again.

I shrugged. "Maybe you had it right the first time."

She cast me a look of exasperation, then tilted her head

and checked the flower motifs. Satisfied that all were centered, she rinsed out her sponge at the sink.

With the water running, she didn't hear when a kettle boiled over on the stove. I jumped up, turned down the burner, and yanked off the lid with a hand wrapped in the tail of my oversized T-shirt. "Pot roast?" I whooped. Then I saw the pan of creamy yellow liquid just starting to bubble. "And lemon pudding? Wow! What's going on? Why the super supper?"

Aunt Queenie wrinkled her nose in distaste. "Supper is such a backwoods expression. You know I prefer to call it dinner."

"Okay, so it's dinner. But red meat and dessert on the same night? Aunt Queenie, I *dream* about meals like this. I even count hamburgers to fall asleep."

"Such melodrama, Delrita. You should be on the stage."

"I'm trying to find out what's up your sleeve."

Her answer was a "wait-and-see" smile.

That might work on an eight-year-old rattling a Christmas present. To me, age fourteen, it was like pouring gasoline on a fire. I opened my eyes wide, as though I'd just figured out one of life's important truths. "Oh, I know," I said, patting my skinny hips. "You've been saying my jeans are falling off. You're afraid I'll drop my drawers tonight at the nursing home."

Aunt Queenie's painted-on eyebrows arched upward. "Well, I declare, Delrita. Drop your drawers! What a thing to say!"

I sat back down at the table and picked up my knife,

pleased at myself for getting a rise out of her. She was always so serious about everything, and I was always trying to loosen her up. You'd think she'd have gotten used to me in seven months, but I could still shock her from the top of that bird's nest to the soles of her purple high-heeled shoes.

Aunt Queenie's real name was Queen Esther, after a famous queen in the Bible, and she sometimes could be a royal pain. For me, getting occasional rises out of her played a part in my survival.

She had no children of her own, but she had me now because Uncle Bert—my mother's brother—was my legal guardian. My being here wasn't a matter of choice for any of us. One minute I was a kid with two loving parents, and the next, I was an orphan.

Orphan. What an ugly word. I'd gladly rip that page from the dictionary, but I still wouldn't have Mom and Dad. Uncle Bert says the Lord doesn't give a person more burdens than he can bear, but I wonder sometimes if there was a mixup of records in heaven. Less than three months after I lost Mom and Dad, I lost Punky, my uncle with Down's syndrome.

Lost. Not an ugly word, but misleading. I didn't *lose* anybody. They just died. Mom and Dad were killed in a car accident last September. Punky's heart, weak since birth, stopped beating last December. Punky was thirty-five years old, but because he'd had the mind of a child, he was more like my little brother than my uncle. The three people I loved most in the world had been taken from me in three months' time, and if that's not a mixup in burden records, I don't know what is.

Mentally, I gave myself a shake, unwilling to let depression get its hooks in me because sometimes it wouldn't let go. I went back to whittling my trumpeter swan and waited for the calming of my soul. Carving could do that for me. I hadn't had much say in anything else that happened in my life, but carving gave me a sense of control.

Like the gouges and V-tools laid out on a folded bath towel before me, my knife was razor sharp—for the simple reason that it's easier to guide a sharp tool than a blunt one. The towel was there to catch the swan, which I would drop if I cut myself. I don't mind bleeding now and then, but I try never to stain the basswood.

The swan's wingspan was only six inches, and its neck was no bigger around than a matchstick. At this stage, I needed to make tiny, precise cuts, so I pulled the knife blade toward me instead of pushing it sharp side out.

My mood had just begun to level off when Aunt Queenie walked over behind me and touched me on the shoulder. "Delrita, I don't know how you do it. That swan looks like any minute it could just take off and fly."

I nodded, scooted wood shavings into a pile with my finger, and wiped my hand on my Levi's.

"It's a shame you aren't sharing your talent with others," she said. "As a member of the advisory board, I'm inviting you to display your carvings at the nursing home."

"No way," I said, easing away from her and the cloying scent of her lilac perfume. Aunt Queenie, so active in community affairs, was used to the spotlight. I never wanted to be the center of attention.

"The residents would enjoy your work," she persisted,

"and the board would appreciate your cooperation. With these new programs, we're bringing the young and the old together, so they can learn from each other."

"Aunt Queenie, what you're doing for the old folks is a good thing. They probably loved the accordion player and that calypso group, and they're sure to love the clown tonight. But do me a favor and forget about me. I'm not interested in showing my wood carvings at the nursing home or anyplace else. I carve for my own enjoyment, *not* to let the whole world know."

"My, aren't you the surly one this afternoon!" she said, brushing a few wood splinters into her palm and heading for the cabinet.

"I'm sorry. It's just that my carving is private and personal, and I'm real choosy about the people I share it with."

"Well, I declare, Delrita. I thought teenagers were concerned with their image, but here you are, still hiding your light under a bushel."

And you're hiding trash under the sink, I mused as she tossed the splinters into the can and closed the cupboard door.

I missed home, where the trash can had sat in plain sight by the stove. I missed the times I'd helped Mom in the kitchen. Aunt Queenie liked for me to do my carving while she cooked, but she seldom needed help from me. Her kitchen was equipped with every appliance known to man.

As if to verify that, she switched on the Dustbuster to clean a few crumbs off the floor. I sighed. I'd been more or less thrown into the lap of luxury when I moved in with her and Uncle Bert. They spoiled me, maybe because I'd lost my parents, or maybe because I was the child they could never have. Or maybe—and this was the biggie—because I was a job they'd been given, and they were determined to do it well.

My thoughts were drawn to the cross-stitched picture hanging above the kitchen phone. *Home is where your loved ones are. It's where you hang your heart.* It was a nice sentiment, but it didn't make everything rosy. That picture was there for looks, like the cold fireplace in the living room.

Aunt Queenie returned the Dustbuster to the utility closet and came out shaking her head. "Pop's messier than a two-year-old, dropping crumbs all over the house. The man spent years in the army, keeping things in tiptop shape, but all of a sudden, he doesn't care about appearances at all. I declare. Sometimes, I think he deliberately tries to make things harder for me."

I glanced at Orvis Roebuck snoozing in the family room, a gorilla in Aunt Queenie's jungle of hanging plants. Beside him on the table was a pack of chewing tobacco. Because he had heart trouble and emphysema, he had to chaw his nicotine instead of puffing cigarettes.

I felt sorry for Mr. Roebuck, but I didn't like him, and he had no use for me. His Sunday visits hadn't been so bad, but then he'd moved in two weeks ago on April Fool's Day. After that, he clammed up and wouldn't talk much to me. However, he always had plenty to say to Aunt Queenie, and it was usually something grouchy. I imagined him staying awake nights, thinking up ways to irritate her. I almost couldn't blame him. In his own house, he'd been the man in charge. In this house, he was a misfit like me.

Aunt Queenie washed her hands, then poured the lemon pudding into a pie crust. "Pop's always been contrary," she said. "It's second nature to him after all his years of giving orders. Since Mama died, he's gotten worse."

If you ask me, he'd gotten worse in the last two weeks. I heard his wheezy muttering, saw him get up and search among the plants. I knew that any second he'd be yelling for his spit can, which Aunt Queenie had hidden in the magazine rack.

Sure enough, he roared, "Queen! Where'd you put it this time?"

"Put what, Pop?"

"My spit can, dad-blame it!"

"Oh, that nasty thing." Aunt Queenie rolled her eyes at me. It was a terrible sacrifice for her to allow him to chew tobacco in the house, and she despised that spit can. Still, the can was better than having him stand at the front door and gob on the porch.

Come to think of it, the spitting could be why he didn't like me. I'd caught him gobbing into Aunt Queenie's prize-winning dieffenbachia, and although I hadn't tattled yet, he never knew when I might. I was keeping an eye on the dieffenbachia, because if it died, Aunt Queenie would have a royal fit.

"Well, where is it?" gargled Mr. Roebuck in the doorway. His left cheek was puckered by a scar, and tobacco juice was dribbling down his chin on that side. His thick gray hair, sheared off in a military cut, stood up like bristles on a brush. He was wearing sharply creased fatigue

pants and a sleeveless undershirt, and his forearms were tat-
tooed—a perfect rose on the left one, and a crudely lettered
"Babe" on the right.

How this man could have fathered Aunt Queenie was
beyond me. I wondered if her mother was "Babe" and if
she'd been some kind of saint to marry him. Saint Babe, the
mother of Queen Esther. The thought made me smile.

"Your spit can's in the magazine rack," Aunt Queenie
said. "You left it by your chair with the lid off again, and
Delrita came within an inch of kicking it over."

"Carelessness," Mr. Roebuck grunted from the good
side of his mouth. "Kids these days have their heads in the
clouds." After sharing that bit of wisdom, he disappeared
into the family room.

With a loud crack, Aunt Queenie demolished an egg on
the edge of the sink, and dumped the whole gooey mess
into the garbage disposal. Wow. It wasn't like her to waste
food—or to lose her cool.

"I hope Tangle Nook gets that new psychiatric hospital," she muttered, breaking another egg and carefully separating the white from the yolk. "I'll be needing it when
Pop drives me nuts."

"Maybe they'll let us share a room," I said.

She grinned at me, and for a moment, I felt a glimmer
of kinship between us—the same kinship we'd had during
Punky's last days of life. When the doctor confessed he
couldn't do anything but keep Punky comfortable in the
hospital, we'd brought him home, where he was sur-
rounded by the belongings he treasured and the people he

loved. Uncle Bert and I had kept watch over Punky, but it was Aunt Queenie who shaved and washed and fed him. Bought him presents. Even arranged for a visit from Santa Claus. Punky died with a smile on his face.

"I hope this works," said Aunt Queenie as she separated another egg.

"You mean the meringue?" I asked.

"I mean the pie and pot roast." She touched the pencil in her hair—a sure sign that she'd been thinking hard on a subject and figuring all the angles.

"Okay, Aunt Queenie. 'Fess up. What's going on in your head?"

Her expression was cagey as she fingered the pencil again. "They say the way to a man's heart is through his stomach, and I intend to get through to Pop. Mama always made a pie when she wanted to sweeten his disposition. Lemon meringue is his favorite."

Why am I not surprised? I thought. Lemon pie for a sour-puss.

Aunt Queenie plugged in her electric mixer with a flourish. "I know it hurt Pop's pride to lose his independence, and pride's always been a big thing with him. I've given him two weeks to get used to us, and he's been a slob the whole time. Since we all have to live under the same roof, I'm going to ask that he make a few concessions."

"Such as?" I said, already sensing the fireworks.

"Such as keeping a civil tongue in his mouth, not spitting on the porch, and not leaving whiskers in the sink. Such as lifting the toilet seat, so he doesn't splatter." With a gleam in her eye, Aunt Queenie turned on the mixer and went after those egg whites like a woman possessed.

I angled my eyes toward her father in the family room. The old man didn't stand a chance.

2

Me and
My Big Mouth

Aunt Queenie dabbed and poked at the meringue on the pie as if she were sculpting a great work of art. She was a perfectionist, born and bred, and once I'd accepted that, living with her had been easier.

We'd had war when Punky and I first came to live here, mainly because I'd been so protective of him, and some of his quirks drove her up the wall. The chicken bones, for instance. To Punky, they were "chinny" bones, and he'd gotten a kick out of flinging them behind the TV.

"Penny for your thoughts," Aunt Queenie said as she slid the pie into the oven to brown the meringue.

"Just thinking about Punky."

Her smile created a net of fine wrinkles at the corners of her eyes. "He poured out my shampoo and scalped all my flowers, but he stole my heart in a thousand ways."

I smiled back at her, then watched her remove cooking utensils from the dishwasher and hang them on the rack—

the long ones on the left and the short ones on the right. Whether it was utensils or community events, organizing things came as natural to her as breathing. Sometimes all that organizing drove *me* up the wall. Tonight, though, she'd arranged for Outrageous the Clown to perform at the nursing home, and I could hardly wait for that.

Outrageous was none other than Trezane Shackleford, Junior, better known as Tree. I was head-over-heels for the big, freckle-faced redhead. Just thinking about him made my heart flutter, so I'd probably go into cardiac arrest when I saw him tonight on stage.

Aunt Queenie finally stopped fussing at the cabinet, fetched her flowered tote bag filled with yarn, and sat down across from me to crochet.

I checked out the color of the yarn on her hook. Light blue. Wonderful. Green was my favorite color, but I didn't want green doilies and doodads popping up in my room.

We worked in comfortable silence—Aunt Queenie adding loops to her project, and me taking away slivers from mine. This is how it should be, I thought. We're at the same table. We're getting along. We're carving out a life together. . . . Whoa, what a clever turn of phrase.

"You know," I said, "we should do this more often."

"What's that?" asked Aunt Queenie, not missing a beat with her loops.

"Work together on our hobbies."

"I didn't take up crochet as a hobby. I want to be productive when I'm tied up in meetings or waiting for the phone to ring at the crisis center."

No wonder she was getting crow's feet around her eyes.

She never let herself relax. "What's that you're working on now?" I asked.

"A baby blanket."

"Oh, wow! Does Uncle Bert know?"

Aunt Queenie's hands stopped moving, and I realized too late that what I'd meant as a joke was a hurtful remark to someone who couldn't have children. "I'm sorry. I—"

"It's for Birthright. They give blankets to new mothers in crisis, usually single women," she said briskly, but beneath the purple eye shadow, her blue eyes flashed with pain.

Me and my big mouth.

The silence was no longer comfortable. It stretched between us, separating us like a huge, gaping chasm. Aunt Queenie sat motionless, staring at her hook, and I knew she'd either lost her place or simply couldn't concentrate. I wanted her to chew me out, lecture me, anything to get her talking.

The stillness dragged on. I listened to the whisper of my knife on the basswood and to my own breathing.

The buzzer going off startled both of us. Aunt Queenie jumped up and lifted the pie from the oven, using her flowered mitts. That bit of activity broke the spell, and when she sat back down to her crochet, she said, "I suppose Avanelle's nervous about tonight."

Avanelle Shackleford was my best friend and Tree's sister, and she was making her debut tonight in the clown act. "She's a total wreck," I said.

"That's only natural. It's first-time jitters, and it'll pass."

"That's what Tree told her, but it didn't help."

"Well, she'll find an appreciative audience at the nursing home," said Aunt Queenie. "Those folks are grateful for anything anyone does for them. Some are terribly lonely because they've outlived their own children. Others have children who've all but forgotten them. That's why Teen Buddies is making such a hit."

Uh-oh. Teen Buddies was a nursing home program that matched old folks with teenagers, one on one. I wanted no part of it. Old folks were depressing, and I could get depressed just fine all by myself. Aunt Queenie could talk me into handing out flyers and collecting donations for worthwhile causes, but she couldn't talk me into being a buddy to a person six times my age. I kept my head down, kept whittling away on my swan.

But my aunt was nothing if not determined. She said, "It gives the elderly a new lease on life when teenagers show an interest in them, whether it's challenging them to a game of checkers or just listening to stories of the past."

Scrape, scrape. Whittle, whittle.

"Becoming a Teen Buddy would give you a sense of fulfillment."

Playing checkers with some old man would give me a good case of down-in-the-dumps, but I managed not to say that. I'd have been home free if Mr. Roebuck hadn't started hacking and spitting in the family room. I frowned in his direction.

Following my gaze, Aunt Queenie said, "You mustn't judge all the elderly by the actions of one person. Please, just keep an open mind while you're in the nursing home. Remember, prejudice can come in many forms."

Prejudice? I wasn't prejudiced! I opened my mouth to

object, then decided it wasn't worth an argument. Maybe I should just clear out of the kitchen for a few minutes.

I could feel Aunt Queenie watching as I packed my woodcarving tools into my old Barbie suitcase, wrapped the swan in tissue paper, and placed it in the shoe compartment. After dumping the shavings into the trash, I came back and rolled up the towel. "I'll set the table in a little bit. I want to put on a clean shirt for tonight."

Aunt Queenie pursed her lips and took stock of my T-shirt and jeans. "A dress would be nice," she said.

She was forever trying to persuade me to wear something besides jeans, but I was self-conscious about being tall and skinny, and my pipe-cleaner legs hardly ever saw daylight. "No dress for me, thanks, but you get two points for trying."

She crossed her arms, like I knew she would. That's how she played the game. "If you weren't such a picky eater, you wouldn't have to hide beneath a sloppy shirt and baggy jeans."

"Who says I'm hiding? Besides, if those folks up at the nursing home are really lonesome, they wouldn't care if I showed up in my nightgown."

"Fine," she said, "but wear a robe that matches."

My laugh was cut short by a car pulling into the driveway. It was Uncle Bert coming home from his real-estate office.

"Is it that time already?" yelped Aunt Queenie, streaking over to peer into the mirror mounted inside a cabinet door. She smoothed her eyebrows with her fingers, then patted her topknot, making sure every hair was lacquered stiff.

I smiled to myself. It was no secret she was older than Uncle Bert. The secret was how much older, and that was as closely guarded as Fort Knox.

She finished at the mirror as Uncle Bert walked in the back door. The new gray suit she'd picked out for him didn't have a wrinkle, but his toupee was slightly off-center. That was typical of Uncle Bert—colored by Aunt Queenie's influence, shaded with his own inelegant style.

"Hello, ladies," he said. "It smells wonderful in here."

"Pot roast and trimmings. Lemon meringue pie," said Aunt Queenie, sweeping across the kitchen and lifting her cheek for a kiss. It was always the left cheek, I'd noticed, so she wouldn't stab him with the pencil.

Uncle Bert smiled down at her. "So this is the night you're gonna sweeten up Orvis, then lower the boom on the old goat."

I giggled at his using Punky's favorite expression, but Aunt Queenie said, "Bert! That's no way to talk!"

He winked at me as he whisked off the toupee, then stashed it on a shelf in the utility closet. In my mind, I saw Punky lifting that toupee and kissing the bald head underneath.

"You're right, Queenie," said Uncle Bert. "He's not an old goat. He's an old rhinoceros—tougher hide. Lucky for me, I won't have to hang around. I've got to show a house to a client later."

"Then we'll talk to Pop right after dinner."

"We?" said Uncle Bert.

"Yes, *we,*" replied Aunt Queenie. "We're a team. Remember?"

"In this case, I'd just as soon you pull the load by yourself. You heard him when I suggested he lower the price of his house. He called me a shyster. Accused me of—"

"Bert, don't worry so much. He's my father, not a potentate. This will be a simple conversation, not out-and-out war."

Uncle Bert raised his eyebrows at me. We both knew nothing was ever simple with Aunt Queenie.

Mr. Roebuck coughed, and all of us stared into the family room, where he had kicked back in his lounge chair to read the paper. His bristly gray hair glistened in the lamplight.

"It's not fair," muttered Uncle Bert.

Aunt Queenie wrinkled her brow at him. "What isn't?"

"All that hair wasted on a grouchy old man."

My room was littered with schoolbooks, a couple of chunks of basswood, and the fuzzy pink house slippers I'd kicked off in a hurry this morning. However, it was basically neat—bed made and clothes put away. Mom had taught me well.

Aunt Queenie, thrilled that I didn't let crud grow under the bed, had declared this room my sanctuary, and despite the pink walls and vanilla carpet, it almost felt like my old room at home. She'd gotten rid of her modern furniture and pink satin accessories. In their place were my sea-green curtains and matching spread, my antique desk, and my great-grandparents' dresser and four-poster bed.

I had only a couple of mementos of my parents—the family photo on my desk, and the God's eye I'd created for them out of yarn and Popsicle sticks in second grade. This reminder that God is always watching over us now hung over the mirror in my bathroom, and it somehow made me feel like my parents were watching over me.

Lined up on the dresser were the clowns I'd carved for Punky, and in the dresser's kneehole sat his little-boy lunch box and basket of peeled crayons. To me, the clean, waxy smell of the crayons was as sweet as potpourri.

That scent gave way to cedar as soon as I opened the closet door. I walked in and stared at my wardrobe. This was a special night, so what should I wear? Something fancier than a T-shirt. Something to complement my string-bean figure. Something Tree couldn't help but notice. My mint-green blouse. The elastic in the waist would fluff out the fabric and add a little fullness to my hips.

As I riffled through the closet, looking for the blouse, I thought how Tree and Avanelle and I had pawed through the racks at the Salvation Army Store, putting his clown costume together—each piece of clothing more ridiculous than the last. We'd laughed so hard, everyone in the store stayed clear of us, and the sour-faced clerk who took Tree's money told us our behavior was "just outrageous."

"That's it!" yelled Tree, slapping the counter. "From here on out, my name's *Outrageous*," and our howling laughter caused two women to beat a hasty retreat from the store.

With a sigh, I pulled the blouse from its hanger. I was crazy about Trezane Shackleford. If only I could tell whether he was attracted to me, or just being his regular friendly self.

In the bathroom, I changed into the blouse, then studied my reflection. Deep-set blue eyes. Small nose and chin. Face too thin. Maybe cutting my hair would have made my face seem fuller, but I couldn't do it. My dad had liked my hair the way it was—straight and long.

Don't most males like long hair? I silently asked the mirror. In the movies, doesn't the guy run his hands through the girl's golden tresses while smothering her with kisses?

I imagined Tree stroking my mousy brown hair and smooching around on me. With a little snort of laughter, I imagined Avanelle gagging if it ever came to that.

3

Two Tomcats
in a Gunnysack

I was filling glasses with ice water in the dining room, but I could hear Aunt Queenie talking to her father.

". . . sell the house," she was saying, "you won't have to worry about the yard work and taxes and repairs."

"Worrying about that house was a danged sight better than having a full-time baby sitter," he countered. " 'Eat this. Drink that. Take your medicine.' I haven't had a minute's peace since I walked in the door."

"Pop, *you* called *me* in the middle of the night, scared you were having a stroke. After that, you *wanted* to move in here with us."

"Thought I was dying, Queen. A man doesn't want to die alone."

"I don't want you to die, period."

"So why are you pampering me to death?"

"Because you need someone to look after you."

I chewed my lower lip. Would it have been so hard to say, "Because I love you, Pop"?

Maybe she didn't love him. I'd thought fathers and daughters were supposed to love each other, no matter what, but Aunt Queenie and Mr. Roebuck were like two tomcats in a gunnysack. It was all so confusing. How could you love someone, yet be so . . . *abrasive* all the time?

Maybe what we had here was a paradox. I'd found that word in my vocabulary book, and I liked the sound of it. Paradox: something that seems to contradict itself.

What if the link connecting Aunt Queenie and her father wasn't love at all? What if he was here because his only other choice was the old folks' home? What if she was taking care of him out of a sense of responsibility?

As I poured the last of the ice water, I suddenly felt cold myself. What if that was the only reason she was taking care of me?

Mr. Roebuck shuffled in and glowered at the table. "Always eating off of china," he muttered, "like a bunch of dad-blamed sissies."

"I'm not a sissy. I'm a shyster," said Uncle Bert, and I couldn't help smiling.

"Whatcha grinnin' at, girlie?" asked Mr. Roebuck as he sat down across from me.

Girlie. Yuk. "Nothing," I mumbled and took my seat. I didn't want to meet his eyes, didn't want to see his perpetual frown, but somehow I couldn't help it. My gaze caught his, like a magnet drawing metal, and his eyes were cold blue steel. I swallowed nervously.

The smell of pot roast, so tantalizing earlier, now made me dread the fireworks that would come after it. I decided to eat fast and excuse myself before dessert.

Uncle Bert asked the blessing, then served up slices of pot roast.

"Just a small one for me," I said.

"What?" squawked Aunt Queenie. "This from the girl who dreams of red meat?"

"I'm sorry. I'm—uh—guess I'm excited about tonight," I said, knowing now I'd have to stick around for the pie.

Aunt Queenie spoke to the ceiling. "I declare. If I make it through these next few years, it'll be a miracle."

"You'll survive," said Mr. Roebuck. "Your mother and I did."

Aunt Queenie clicked her lavender nails on the table. "And just what is that supposed to mean?"

"Nothing, Queen. Forget it."

"No, I won't. I was a quiet girl, Pop. We didn't live in one place long enough for me to make a lot of friends and be a normal teenager."

"That's not the time I'm talking about. It was later."

"Later?"

"When you met *him*," said Mr. Roebuck, jerking his head toward Uncle Bert. "He was too young. You were robbing the cradle."

That struck a nerve. Aunt Queenie made a strangling noise, and her rouged cheeks blossomed a deep rose red.

"Orvis," barked Uncle Bert, "that old horse was beaten to death twelve years ago when we got married, and I won't stand for you bringing it up again."

The old man held his hands in front of him as if to ward off blows. "Hey, Bert, don't get excited. Queen's mother was upset by the age difference, but it didn't bother me a bit. Forget I mentioned it."

Uncle Bert glared at him for a few seconds, then served himself some roast.

Aunt Queenie had regained her composure. Passing a bowl to her father, she said, "Save room for pie, Pop. It's your favorite."

"Didn't ask for no pie," the old man replied as he shoveled mashed potatoes onto his plate. "I did ask that you stay out of my room. Don't want you in there going through my things."

"I didn't go through your things. I simply tidied up."

Mr. Roebuck jammed the spoon into the potatoes and thrust the bowl at me. Then he pointed a finger at his daughter. "You messed with my duffel bag, knocked it over. From now on, I'm stashing it away where you won't have to look at it."

"That's fine with me," said Aunt Queenie. "It's practically a rag."

"Well, it's *my* rag," muttered Mr. Roebuck, "and I want you to leave it alone."

I couldn't bear their arguing all the way through dinner, so I said the only thing I could think of: "Aunt Queenie,

Avanelle's mom wasn't able to shorten the sleeves on that shirt. If she'd cut the thread that holds the sequins, they'd have come unstrung."

Uncle Bert stopped chewing to stare at Aunt Queenie. "You gave away your sequined shirt?"

"I did. It's been hanging in the closet for three years. I haven't touched it since the garden club threw that New Year's Eve party."

"But you were beautiful in that shirt."

"Well, I declare, Bert," said Aunt Queenie, blushing to the roots of her straw-blond hair. "You could have told me before. It's too late now. It would hurt Avanelle's pride if I asked for it back."

"It probably would," he agreed, "and that family's already had too many blows to its pride."

"It's the father's fault," said Orvis Roebuck. "Hardworking citizens had to support his family while he served time in prison."

I dropped my fork, and it clattered on my plate. "Please don't ever say that to Avanelle. She doesn't need someone throwing that prison business in her face."

"I know that, girlie. I don't blame *her.*"

"Pop, you're being too judgmental," said Aunt Queenie. "Mr. Shackleford served several months for a crime he didn't commit. Gardenia didn't like living on welfare, but she had no choice—not with seven children, and one of them a new baby."

Mr. Roebuck ignored her. "There's no justice in this world," he went on. "Those kids have got a dad they can't depend on, and the girlie here doesn't have one at all. It don't seem right to me."

I stared into my water glass. I'd had the same thought a time or two, right after my parents were killed, and I still felt ashamed of it. But the old man had his nerve, saying such a thing. He didn't care whether I had a dad or not. He just didn't like me living in this house.

"Gardenia and the kids are a fine family," said Uncle Bert, "and my impression of Trezane is that he's a good man. He was in church the first Sunday after his parole, and he's looking for work. That could be a struggle in a town like Tangle Nook, Missouri, because guilty or not, he's got a criminal record. Employers might be leery of hiring him."

"I would, if it was me," said Mr. Roebuck.

"Well, I declare, Pop," said Aunt Queenie. "You're behaving like a typical old goat."

My eyes popped. She'd disapproved of Punky and Uncle Bert using that term, and here she was using it herself. Orvis Roebuck must be pushing her over the edge.

"I just call 'em like I see 'em," he said.

I turned to Uncle Bert. "You helped Mrs. Shackleford find that house to rent, and you shamed the landlord into fixing the place up. Maybe you could help Mr. Shackleford find a job."

"I doubt it. I can hire him now and then to paint a house before I put it on the market. Beyond that, there's not much I can do."

When Aunt Queenie got up to serve the pie, I poured

coffee for the grownups. As soon as we were seated, she shook out her linen napkin and said, "Pop, Bert and I have something to discuss with you."

Orvis Roebuck grunted. "Sounds serious. Whatever's on your mind, just spit it out."

Spit, as in tobacco juice. Forcing myself not to think of that, I took a bite of pie.

Aunt Queenie said, "All families have problems—"

"And we've got a truckload of 'em," interrupted her father. "For one, a man can't have his privacy. I'm gonna stick a sign on my door: 'Stay out of my room and leave my gear alone.' "

"Don't be ridiculous, Orvis," said Uncle Bert. "Queenie has every right to go in there and clean."

Mr. Roebuck scowled at him. "I can run a sweeper and make a bed. I did it at home."

"How often did you change the sheets, Pop?" asked Aunt Queenie.

"When I thought about it. What difference does it make? Nobody slept on them but me."

She winced in disgust. "Get used to it, Pop. I'll be cleaning your room and changing your sheets once a week. I will, however, leave your duffel bag untouched."

"Hmmmmph."

Aunt Queenie sipped her coffee, replaced the cup in the saucer, and plucked the pencil from her topknot. "Okay, Pop," she said, "I've listened to your complaints. Now you listen to mine. I know it's difficult for you, living in a home that's not your own. I've tried to be patient, but my patience is wearing thin. You seem to have lost your sense of pride, and some of your habits have given me pause."

"Given you pause?" Mr. Roebuck snorted. "What kind of talk is that? There's nothing wrong with my habits. Queen, you've always been a prissy little thing, and now you're getting worse. Have you forgotten that this is retired Master Sergeant Orvis Roebuck here, not some snotty-nosed kid?"

I laid down my fork, because with all this talk about spit and snot, I felt like throwing up.

"So where's the man who once presented such a fine figure in uniform?" prodded Aunt Queenie. "Where's the man who provided for Mama and me and treated us with respect? Where's the man who came home with medals from World War Two?"

That's the very subject we were studying in history class. We won that war, in spite of Mr. Roebuck.

He narrowed his eyes at Aunt Queenie. "You know nothing about World War Two," he said. "You weren't even born yet."

"I've seen your pictures, and the medals, too."

"Don't wanna talk about that."

"That's your choice." Aunt Queenie twiddled the pencil between her fingers, and my eyes met Uncle Bert's. We nodded at each other, almost imperceptibly. A jiggling pencil meant both barrels were loaded, ready to fire.

"Now, about those habits, Pop." Stabbing the pencil at the table, Aunt Queenie ticked off her grievances: ". . . whiskers on the sink . . . splatters on the toilet seat . . . lid off the sugar bowl . . . spitting on the porch."

Mr. Roebuck's face was a glob of wrinkles and puckers and bulging eyes. He slammed down his fist, and the dishes rattled. "Queen, I made a career out of defending this country. I've given orders to soldiers and taken orders from my superiors, and I'll be dad-blamed if I'll start taking orders from a daughter who's twenty-six years younger than I am!"

The pencil dropped from Aunt Queenie's hand and pinged against her coffee cup. She glanced quickly at me, then at Uncle Bert, her face a mask of shock. I did some quick mental calculation. If Mr. Roebuck was seventy-four, she was forty-eight, *fifteen years* older than Uncle Bert.

After a couple of heartbeats, Aunt Queenie picked up the pencil and tapped it on the table. Smooth as silk, she said, "I hardly think asking someone to be neat about his person is giving orders, but call it what you will. When I was a child, you told me I would follow your rules as long as I lived in your house. The circumstances are different, but the rules are the same. You will behave like a gentleman as long as you live in *my* house."

Mr. Roebuck burst into a coughing fit, which I suspected was deliberate, so he'd have time to think. When he had control of himself again, he croaked, "Supposing I clean up after myself a little better, Queen, will you do something for me?"

"What's that, Pop?"

He scooted back his chair and clambered to his feet. "Loosen up, and stop acting like a dad-blamed, old-maid schoolmarm with her underwear in a twist."

Aunt Queenie gasped, and her father stomped out of the room.

"Well, I declare. I just declare." Aunt Queenie inserted the pencil in her hair with enough force to flatten a tire, then flounced away from the table.

Uncle Bert sat glaring in the direction of his father-in-law. "Ungrateful old coot," he said, clenching and unclenching his hands on the tablecloth. "I'd set him up in his own little apartment if I could. But I can't. We're his family. We're all he's got left."

The dab of food I'd eaten lay heavy in my stomach. How I wished I could roll back the clock, clear back to September, when "family" meant having Mom and Dad and Punky.

4

A Man of
Few Words

Uncle Bert and I carried the dirty dishes into the kitchen, where Aunt Queenie was polishing the stove top. The lemony smell of appliance wax mingled with the lilac scent of her perfume.

As I rinsed plates under the faucet, Uncle Bert tried to reassure Aunt Queenie. "What you said in there was true, hon, so hold your ground and don't let the old man get you down."

No answer.

I turned and saw my aunt's flushed face, saw her eyes brimming with tears.

Uncle Bert stood for a moment, looking helpless, then loaded plates into the dishwasher. "I'll never understand how a man like Orvis could have produced a child like you. Mother Nature sure got her wires crossed on that one."

Still no answer.

"Queenie, listen to me," said Uncle Bert. "You're not

an old-maid schoolmarm. You're a beautiful woman, and I'm proud to have you for my wife."

She still didn't say anything, but I thought her polishing hand might take the paint off the stove.

My dislike for Orvis Roebuck grew. Maybe Aunt Queenie wasn't the easiest person in the world to live with, but we'd been perking along fairly well until *he* moved in. How dare he insult her and make her cry.

Uncle Bert added the detergent and pushed the START button on the dishwasher. "Queenie, hon," he said, "I hate to run off when you're upset, but it's time for Delrita and me to hit the road."

She nodded.

I picked up the purse and jeans jacket I'd left on a chair. Uncle Bert told Aunt Queenie good-bye and kissed her on the cheek. As he fetched his briefcase and toupee from the closet, she finally spoke. "Delrita, you'll call when you're ready to come home?"

"I'll call."

She patted my shoulder, I kissed the air near her face, and we stood for a moment in awkward silence. She was waiting for a hug that I was never quite able to give.

For some people, hugging is easy. For me, it's not. I have to feel loved first. I have to have a place to hang my heart.

Lacking that, I was keeping Queen Esther Holloway at a distance. I wouldn't let myself hug the queen.

"I can't believe I gave up my space out here for that old goat," said Uncle Bert as we walked through the garage. "If he was half as meticulous about his habits as he is with that truck, Queenie wouldn't have extra work."

I glanced over at Mr. Roebuck's sporty red pickup. Even in the dimness of the garage, its newly waxed surface gleamed.

Uncle Bert's five-year-old Lincoln Continental filled the driveway like a huge white ship at berth. We climbed aboard, and Uncle Bert reminded me to buckle up. Ever since the accident that killed my parents, he'd been a stickler for safety belts.

As soon as we cleared the driveway, he said, "Orvis made a big blunder when he revealed Queenie's age."

"She sure doesn't look forty-eight."

"No, she doesn't, and I hope you'll keep that number to yourself. It's nobody's business that she's older than I am, and I don't want you spreading it around."

"I wouldn't do that," I said, feeling a little bit insulted. I stared out the window, seeing nothing, until we came to my father's antique shop. I turned away quickly, but not before I'd read the sign on the door: NEW OWNERS.

Just two little words, but they hurt so much.

The nursing home, Tangle Nook Rest Haven, was a one-story building with so many additions, it sprawled across one whole block. The flag out front waved gently in the glow of upturned floodlights. It made me think of Punky, who never passed Old Glory without snapping a salute.

Uncle Bert dropped me off at the canopied main entrance, then called out the window as he pulled away, "If you get lost in the maze, just climb up one of Queenie's rubber trees and scout your way out."

I waved at him and opened one of the double glass doors.

A mixture of smells greeted me—disinfectant, liniment, boiled potatoes, and another vaguely familiar scent that I couldn't quite put my finger on.

In the foyer, soft lights cast an eerie glow over the leaves and branches of a dozen potted plants. A huge aquarium bubbled, its water magnifying the eyes of iridescent tropical fish. The blue chairs on both sides of the hallway were empty, and so was the nurses' station straight ahead. The place seemed spooky, like a hospital without patients, as if all the old folks had died.

I walked toward the hum of voices coming from down the hall. Suddenly, a wheelchair shot out of a connecting hallway and blocked my path. "You can't run away from me," said the driver, a tiny woman in a flowered duster with a lap robe on her knees.

"I—What?" I said, focusing on the pink scalp beneath her wispy white hair.

The woman cackled. "Trying to slip away, weren't you, Liza? You ran off and left me to do the mending, and now I'm gonna tell."

"I—I—"

"Don't mind Gertrude," said another woman, who materialized from that same hallway. The name tag on her uniform identified her as Mrs. Betty Norton, licensed practical nurse. She took hold of the handles at the back of Gertrude's chair and smiled at me. "She gets confused sometimes. I told her we were going to see a clown, and she thought she was a little girl again."

"Oh," I said. "I'm here to see the clown, too, but I don't know where to go."

"Then come along with us," said Mrs. Norton.

"Thanks," I said, falling into step beside the wheelchair.

Gertrude reached out and took my hand. "You have such pretty hands, an artist's hands."

"I—well—I guess I am an artist. I do woodcarving." Now, why had I said that?

"Whittling? I didn't know you could whittle, Liza. Why haven't you whittled something for me?"

"I'm sorry, but I'm not Liza. I'm Delrita Jensen."

"Oh," said the nurse, "your aunt Queenie's told me about you. We certainly appreciate her. She's just brimming with ideas to keep our residents happy."

"I know. She's the one who booked the clown."

"And paid for him, too, because our activity fund is bankrupt. Well, here we are," Mrs. Norton said as she wheeled Gertrude into a dining hall.

I thanked her and stopped beside an empty table. All the other tables had been pushed against a wall to make room for the elderly people seated in chairs and wheelchairs. A few folks were talking, but most were staring vacantly.

Every face I saw had a fragile network of lines, like the cracks in an antique cup. The scent I hadn't been able to identify was potent here, and it hit me that it reminded me of Orvis Roebuck. It was the smell of ancient furniture, of clothes long stored in a trunk, of books in a box in the attic. It was the smell of old age.

"Hi, Delrita."

I turned around—and burst out laughing. Walking toward me was a stack of boxes, complete with a head and a pair of legs. The head had a freckled face, emerald eyes, and a mop of carrot-colored curls that shimmered like fire in the bright light. Avanelle. She was two weeks older than I, but small enough to pass for two years younger.

"Hey, I'm the straight man," she said with pretended peevishness. "You're not supposed to laugh at—" The boxes wobbled, and the tape recorder on top came sliding off.

I caught it, and Avanelle said, "Thanks. Tree'd kill me if that got broken," as she plunked the boxes down on the table.

"Can't say as I'd blame him." Tree'd been clowning for a couple of months, but now that he had the tape recorder *and* Avanelle, he'd come up with a whole new show.

"You'd never blame him for anything," she said. "Tree could rob a bank, and you'd just say he needed money."

"Probably," I admitted, then glanced around. "Where is he?"

"Changing clothes. We're running late because of Gordy. He wandered off, Dad was at a meeting, and Mom couldn't leave the baby."

I grinned and shook my head. At the Shackleford house, there was never a dull moment. Seven kids. Seven green-eyed, redheaded moptops. Tree was the oldest at fifteen, and Ellie, the baby, was only five months.

After removing her old gray sweater that was too long in the front and too short in the back, Avanelle pirouetted so I could see her outfit—the sequined shirt with the sleeves rolled up, the black stirrup pants I'd outgrown, the sparkly bow in her hair.

I whistled.

"Snazzy, isn't it?" she said. The light in her eyes revealed a self-confidence she never had at school in her worn-out jeans and shirts. "When I saw myself in the mirror, I thought, What a gorgeous girl."

"Then you're not scared anymore?"

"Are you kidding? I'm scared spitless."

"I'm a little nervous myself," I confessed.

"You should be. If this show bombs, we're both in trouble."

"Not me," I said. "All I did was offer a few ideas."

Avanelle tapped the tape recorder. "And provide a few sound effects."

"What can I say? I play a mean washboard."

We giggled about that and talked some more. Soon I gave her a thumbs-up and scanned the room, looking for a place to sit. A few rows back, I saw an empty seat and headed toward it.

I was the center of attention as I wove my way around wheelchairs, slippered feet, canes, and crutches. The words "Who's that?" rippled from one person to another. One old man with liver spots on his hand saluted me, and a woman caught my wrist and said, "Hello, doctor."

I smelled urine and saw a puddle by her feet. "I—I'm not a doctor," I said, flustered, and moved on, intent on the empty chair.

I plopped down on it, then jerked my head back in surprise when a hand thrust a teddy bear in my face. Short, stubby fingers had hold of the bear by the neck.

Cautiously, I glanced around, expecting to see a little old lady, and saw a . . . chubby boy.

My heart twisted. I was sure he was mentally retarded. That broad, blank face. That lower lip sticking out too far to keep the tongue in his mouth and stop the drool. Those strange blue eyes that weren't on the same track. One eye was fixed on me, while the other was wallowing in its socket.

The boy was wearing jeans and a red western shirt. The Elvis on his silver belt buckle was partly hidden by the folds of his fat belly, and the plastic envelope in his shirt pocket was jammed full of Magic Markers. Everything about him seemed out of whack, imperfect, except for his amber-colored curls.

He blinked twice at me and grinned, and only then did I realize I was staring. Why couldn't I stop looking at his eyes?

"Is—is this seat taken?" I stammered.

"Ya," he said gruffly. The word had a curious, clipped sound, and I guessed he had a speech defect.

"I'm sorry." I started to rise, but he twisted the bear's head side to side, as if to say "no."

"Oh, I get it," I said. "The seat's taken because I'm in it."

"Ya." He set the raggedy brown bear on his lap, its one eye facing front. Its head sagged onto the red bandanna that was tied around its neck.

The boy's stubby fingers reminded me of Punky's, and

the sight of his bear filled me with an unexpected sadness. Was it that the bear was misshapen like its owner? With only one good eye? Or was it something else?

The boy blinked at me again and pointed at his bear. "Peanut."

"Hello, Peanut. I'm Delrita."

"Weeta?" the boy echoed.

"Yes," I said. "Do you have a name?"

"Ya."

I waited, but the boy just grinned at me.

"Joey's a man of few words," said a dark-haired woman I hadn't noticed before, seated in a wheelchair. When she wiped the drool from his chin with a tissue, I saw that her hand was curved like a claw and had horribly swollen knuckles.

"M-m-my m-m-mama," Joey said, stuttering violently over the m's.

"Yes, I'm the mama." The woman chuckled. "Lucille Marcum. Joey's my son, and he lives here with me."

"But you—you're not that old," I said.

Mrs. Marcum chuckled again. "Joey and I are both older than we look. He's twenty-three, and I'm fifty-eight, which makes me a spring chicken in this place. Rheumatoid arthritis got the best of me, so we had to move in here about a month ago."

I glanced at Joey. He might be older than he looked, but he was much too young for an old folks' home.

"Joey's adjusted better than I have to our change in lifestyle," Mrs. Marcum said. "He's already made friends with everybody here, and he's started working, too."

"At the sheltered workshop," I said.

"Why, yes. How—"

"My uncle worked there."

"Oh. Queenie Holloway told me all about the workshop—how it helps people like Joey become productive members of society. She convinced me he should give it a try."

"That's my aunt Queenie. She gave my mom the same talk about my uncle. Turned out she was right."

"Is your uncle working now?"

"No. He died just before Christmas."

"I'm sorry, hon. How did it happen?"

"His heart."

"Joey's got heart problems, too," Mrs. Marcum said with a tender glance at him. "In fact, he was born with so many things wrong, we didn't expect him to live. I caught German measles when I was carrying him, and I'm afraid he paid the price."

I nodded, unsure of what to say.

"But he's doing pretty good right now," she went on. "His heart hasn't acted up for several months, and that's why I let him try the workshop. I can see the job is good for him, but I worry every day while he's gone, and I watch the clock until he walks through the door."

Joey slapped me on the arm and stuck his legs out straight to show me a pair of cowboy boots. They were little-boy-sized, bright red.

"Wow!" I said. "Those are sharp."

"Ya."

"He bought those boots with his first paycheck," said

Mrs. Marcum. "I tried to talk him into buying black, but he wouldn't have anything but red."

"Just like my uncle," I said, smiling at Joey, who was fiddling with the bandanna on Peanut's neck.

All at once, my eyes misted. The red plaid fabric on the bear's paws had triggered a memory of a teddy bear sitting in the rocking chair in Grandma's old farmhouse. Mom's bear. The one she'd had since she was a little girl.

"Delrita, is something the matter?" asked Mrs. Marcum.

"I just realized Joey's bear is exactly like one my mother had."

"I expect thousands of kids had those bears. They were popular many years ago."

"But Joey's only twenty-three. Mom was thirty-seven."

"Was?" said Mrs. Marcum. "Hon, you don't mean your mother—"

"She and my dad were killed in a car accident. That's why I live with Aunt Queenie."

"Dear me, child. I don't know what to say."

I shrugged. Nothing anybody could say would change anything.

"I'm so sorry," said Mrs. Marcum. "As for Joey's bear, my niece gave him her old one. She's about the age of your mother."

"Oh." I closed my eyes and tried to think. When Uncle Bert was emptying our house in town, he'd offered to put my parents' antiques and personal belongings in storage, but I wouldn't hear of it. I'd wanted *everything* shipped out, sold off, out of my sight.

Gone were the highboy, the round oak table, Mom's

china cabinet with the curved glass doors, and more. But the last time I'd seen that teddy bear and rocking chair had been at the farmhouse. They hadn't showed up at our house in town.

So whatever happened to Mom's bear?

5

Outrageous

I was still puzzling about Mom's bear when a lady moved to the front of the room and called for everyone's attention. "Here's what we've all been waiting for," she said. "The show that's billed as 'Absolutely Outrageous.' So sit back and relax. Our guests are here to put smiles on your faces and songs in your hearts."

"This is it, Joey," I whispered. "You're about to see the neatest clown."

"Ya," he replied, clapping his hands.

I felt myself grinning foolishly as Tree shuffled, barefoot, to center stage. He'd transformed himself into a bashful hillbilly in a battered felt hat, a flour-sack shirt, and overalls so baggy that the crotch came to his knees. The white paint on his face darkened at the jaw with a smudge of charcoal whiskers, and his smile revealed blacked-out front teeth. Give him a rifle and a flop-eared hound, and he could have posed for an Ozarks postcard.

Beside him, in stark contrast, Avanelle glittered like a shooting star as she skipped daintily along.

"Howdy, folks," drawled Tree, tipping his hat to the crowd. "Outrageous is the name. Foolishness is the game. This little gal beside me is called Gimme, 'cause that's what she's here for—to gimme that box, gimme those tennis balls, gimme that deck of cards."

Polite laughter burbled across the room.

"Gimme," said Tree to Avanelle, "ain't that just the most pitiful sounding hee-haw you ever heard?"

"Yup. Like a bunch of mules with the bellyache."

Tree rocked back on his heels and tucked his thumbs into the bib of his overalls. "Reckon we can remedy that?"

"Reckon we can try. Why not tell them about your rabbit?"

"Now there's an idea. Gimme those two boxes over there."

She did, and he said, "Folks, I got me a rabbit so fast, it can outrun a bullet. It's so fast, it can't be seen by the naked eye. I call my rabbit Puff, 'cause you won't see nothin' but a puff of smoke when he takes off out of one box and lands in the other. Now y'all watch closely."

Avanelle lifted the lids, and Tree addressed the box in his left hand: "Ready when you are, Puff. Puff? *Puff!*" His last puff was a huge breath of air that caused the talcum powder in the box to rise up in a cloud. Before the crowd had time to react, he puffed at the talcum powder in the second box.

Back and forth the "rabbit" went, hopping from one box

to the other, while Tree puffed and coughed and hacked at the dust.

The crowd's laughter was loud and genuine, and it lasted until Avanelle slapped the box lids into place.

"Whooo-eeee," hollered Tree. "Did you see that rabbit?"

"Didn't see a thing," yelled an old man up front.

"That's what I've been telling y'all. This rabbit is *fast.*"

More laughter from the crowd.

For twenty minutes or so, Tree kept up his momentum, juggling, doing sleight-of-hand tricks, telling Ozarks jokes.

Joey stared, entranced, all during the performance, as if Tree were clowning just for him. His eyes sparkled, and when he wasn't clapping his hands with glee, he was squeezing Peanut's neck.

Too soon it was time for the finale, and Avanelle set up the tape recorder.

"Folks," Tree said, "it's been pure pleasure for me to tickle your fancies this evening. Before I go, I want to play y'all a song. You might say this is a song from my heart—and from my head and my feet—'cause those are the instruments I'll be using. Just gimme a minute so I can tune up."

With that, Tree rubbed his hand three times across his springy red curls, and the noise we heard—coming from the tape recorder—was that of a saw cutting wood.

The audience loved it.

"Now for my heart," Tree said. He pounded his broad chest, and we heard the hollow, hooting sound that comes from blowing across the top of an empty soda bottle.

Again, the audience laughed.

"And finally, I'll tune up my feet." Tree danced a jig, but instead of hearing the slap of his bare feet, we heard the clank-clank-clank of a spoon being dragged over a washboard.

"Whoo-eeee, I sure sound good," he said. "Now, I'll put all these together, and what'll we have? Music!"

As the tape recorder cranked out a rasping, hooting, clanking rendition of "Oh, Suzannah," Tree, in an amazing display of coordination, rubbed his head, patted his stomach, and tapped his feet all at the same time.

Even before the song ended, the applause and whistling began—and continued while Tree and Avanelle took their bows and ran from the room, hand in hand.

After the clapping died down, the audience stirred, preparing to leave.

Not Joey. He was staring at the door, as if willing Outrageous to come back.

"That was wonderful," said Mrs. Marcum. "I haven't laughed like that in years. Delrita, who are those kids? The girl, especially, seems awfully young."

"They're Tree and Avanelle Shackleford. He's fifteen. She's fourteen."

"Shackleford? I think I know the family. Don't they rent a house over behind McDonald's and have a bunch of kids?"

"Yes," I said, waiting for her to make the connection, to comment about Mr. Shackleford having been in prison.

"I lost track of Joey one day, and I found him playing

with that batch of little redheads," she said. "It was a pleasant surprise. Some kids are cruel to Joey."

I nodded. The Shacklefords had played with Punky, too, as if he were a child and not a man thirty-five years old.

"It was nice meeting you, Delrita," said Mrs. Marcum, extending a twisted hand.

I shook it, oh, so gently. "You, too."

Joey came awkwardly to his feet, and since one leg was shorter than the other, his left shoulder hung lower than his right. He was grinning and holding his hand up.

"Give me five," I said, and we slapped palms, like they do at the sheltered workshop.

"Delrita, I hope you'll come back and see us sometime," said Mrs. Marcum.

I looked around at all the decrepit bodies shuffling off to their rooms. I smelled the scent of old age. This place was depressing, and I didn't really want to come back here. But Joey was peering at me intently with his one good eye. "I—well—I—okay," I said.

"We'll look forward to it. Now, son, will you drive me back to our room?"

"Ya."

I watched as Joey set Peanut on his mother's lap and released the brake on the wheelchair. I noticed him standing taller, now that he had an important job to do.

"Joey," I said, "I'm pretty good friends with Outrageous. Maybe I could bring him, too."

"Ya." With a rocking, side-to-side gait, the man of few words began rolling his mother across the room.

I listened to the bright red cowboy boots clomping against the tile. An idea was taking shape in my mind. If I could have Joey for a partner, being a Teen Buddy wouldn't be half bad.

6

A Carefully
Plotted Scheme

"Well, Velveeta, did we pass?" asked Tree when he and Avanelle returned for their props.

Their little sister, Birdie, had hung that name on me, and every time Tree used it, I felt a fluttering in my chest. "You were tremendous."

"Not tremendous—outrageous," he said, then grinned to show his "missing" teeth.

"Believe it or not," said Avanelle, "once I got started, it was a piece of cake."

Tree threw up his hands. "I've been telling you that for a week, but you never listen to me. What a doofus!"

"Call me that again," she snapped, "and you'll be back to a one-man show."

"So sorry, sis." Tree leaned toward her and smacked his lips. "Let's kiss and make up."

"Get away from me, you jerk."

He looked at me with mock distress. "Velveeta, say it isn't so. Say I'm not a jerk."

"Only if you'll do me a favor. I met a man tonight. Joey Marcum. And I sort of promised I'd bring you back for a visit sometime."

"No prob," said Tree. "He's cool."

"You know Joey?"

"Outrageous knows all."

"Baloney. Joey was at Special Olympics last week," Avanelle said, referring to the Saturday sports program for people with disabilities.

"Then why didn't I see him?" I asked.

"His mom kept him on the bleachers," said Tree. "She's afraid he'll have a heart attack."

"It wouldn't hurt him to toss a basketball or throw a Frisbee."

Tree adjusted his floppy hat. "Try telling that to his mom."

"Maybe I will someday. I'm thinking about signing up to be his Teen Buddy."

"Last I heard, you wanted no part of that program," Avanelle said as she donned the short-tailed sweater. "So what happened?"

"I met Joey."

Tree grinned at me, then glanced at the clock. "Hey, girls, whaddaya say we go to McDonald's for a Coke? I've got the bucks, 'cause they paid me in cash."

"I'm not going anywhere in this getup," said Avanelle. "Just give me my part of the money."

My heart was turning somersaults. Tree had actually invited me someplace. Never mind that he was in costume. Never mind that the people at McDonald's would be staring at us the whole time. This was my big chance, and I didn't want to miss it. I peeled off my jeans jacket and tossed it to Avanelle. "Here. This'll reach clear to your knees. Let me find a phone and get Aunt Queenie's okay."

Praying that Aunt Queenie wouldn't say no, I made the call.

"Walk to McDonald's in the dark?" she said, as if this were some crime-ridden city, instead of Tangle Nook, Missouri. She was determined to take good care of me, or die trying.

"Please, Aunt Queenie. There are three of us, and it's only a few blocks."

"But it's a school night."

"I never go to bed before ten."

Silence. A long silence. Finally, she relented. "Oh, all right. I'll pick you up at nine."

"How about nine-fifteen?"

"Well, I declare, Delrita. Give you an inch, and you'll take a mile."

"Sorry."

"I suppose it's better that you don't come home yet anyway. Pop's out of sorts again."

"I thought he promised to do better."

"To be neater, not nicer. I guess I shouldn't expect too much all at once. After you left, he read something in the paper that set him off. Something about D-Day. It's been more than half a century since the Allies stormed the beaches at Normandy, but you'd think it was yesterday, the way he's carrying on."

"Tell him the war's over. And thanks, Aunt Queenie. See you at nine-fifteen."

Tree and Avanelle were waiting for me in the foyer.

"I can go," I said, so we picked up the boxes and headed outside, where I eased myself into position between my friends. The night air was cool on my bare arms, and heavy with the odor of diesel exhaust, but I didn't mind.

Tree doffed his hat as we passed the flagpole. I smiled. I'd never seen a clown salute the flag before.

"This was the first gig I've had that wasn't a birthday party," he said. "Old folks make a good audience—easy to please."

Avanelle jabbed me in the ribs with her elbow. "He obviously doesn't know much about Mr. Roebuck."

"I know he's got a fine set of wheels," Tree said. "What I wouldn't give to drive that little pickup. Maybe I'll get on his good side and—"

"Mr. Roebuck doesn't have a good side," said Avanelle. "All I've seen is grouchy. The other day, we didn't know he was taking a nap, and he just about bit our heads off for laughing."

"She's right," I said. "Makes me want to sit him down and say, 'Hey, what's your *problem?*' "

"Why don't you?" asked Tree.

"Yeah, right. He'd stand me in front of a firing squad and order me shot."

"I'm serious," Tree persisted. "It's always better to get things out in the open."

"Telephone, television, and tell-a-Tree," sighed Avanelle. "The fastest ways to spread the news. This is the boy who announced to the whole football team that Dad was in prison."

"Well, it worked, didn't it?" said her brother. "It was better than worrying every second that they'd find out. The guys told me they were sorry, slapped me on the back, and hustled on out to play football. It was no big deal. I like talking straight to people. You find out what makes them tick."

"Mr. Roebuck's always ticked about something," I said, and they both groaned at my pun. "At the moment, it's D-Day. At supper, it was his duffel bag. Before that, his spit can."

Tree said, "Maybe he had a horrible experience during the war that he can't forget. Maybe he's got that stress whatcha-call-it problem like some of the Vietnam veterans."

"He was in World War Two," I said, "not Vietnam."

Tree shrugged. "Same difference if you're being shot at."

The diesel exhaust was giving way to burgers and fries, and Avanelle said, "That smell makes me hungry."

"Hey, I'll spring for the Cokes," said Tree, "but it's every man for himself if you want grub."

I knew Avanelle would do without, because she was saving up for Reeboks. She worked two afternoons a week, lady-sitting with Miss Myrtle Chambers from church, and now she'd be making money from the clown act. Her family's backyard connected to the McDonald's parking lot, but she'd vowed not to spend one cent on a Big Mac until she was wearing those new sneakers.

When we turned the corner, we were in sight of her house. In the glow from the living room, the gleaming white of the front porch rails reminded me of a long-toothed grin. The place had been a dump when Mrs. Shackleford and the kids moved in, but the landlord had spruced it up, and he was furnishing the materials to convert the screened-in back porch into a third bedroom.

Through a front window, I saw Mr. Shackleford peeking over the top of a newspaper at two-year-old Gordy, who was bouncing on his lap. I smiled. Mr. Shackleford's eyebrows were brown and bushy as caterpillars, and when he wiggled them just right, he could make the caterpillars walk.

"Dad's been checking the want ads every night, but nothing's turned up yet," whispered Avanelle. "Without a car, he can't go very far for a job, and without a job, he can't fix the car."

I glanced at the hulk in the driveway that was a beat-up station wagon. It hadn't moved for a week, since some guy towed it home.

Through the partially open front door came the sounds of thumping, banging, laughing, crying, and Mrs. Shackleford calling, "Birdie, bring me a diaper."

"Did she poop *again?*" piped Birdie, whose real name was Gilberta.

"Let's leave these props in the yard and split," hissed Tree. "If the gang hears us, they'll buzz out here and stick to us like bugs on flypaper."

At McDonald's, several people recognized Tree, despite the grease paint and hillbilly garb.

"Hey, Shack," called one of three guys in a booth.

"That's not Shack. That's Ronald McDonald," said another.

"Hi, Tree," said some giggly girls in line at the counter. Ninth-graders, all but one. I clenched my teeth when I saw the new girl, Heidi Grissom. Why hadn't she stayed in Arkansas?

She laughed at Tree and waved at me, so I had to wave back.

Avanelle grabbed my arm and pulled me toward the dining area. "Let Tree get the drinks. This is so-o-o embarrassing."

After we slid into a booth, I sat glaring at Heidi, an eighth-grader who'd moved to Tangle Nook three weeks ago. Round pink cheeks and a cloud of curly blond hair gave her the appearance of a happy cherub, but my feelings toward her were not angelic. I resented her because she lived with her grandparents, who'd bought my house and my dad's antique shop. They were three strangers, intruding on my memories, and that little sign, NEW OWNERS, was to me just dirty words.

Every time I saw Heidi, the pain was fresh and new, but it was impossible to avoid her, because she had art, PE, lunch, and math with Avanelle and me. She knew about my parents, and she bent over backward to be nice to me. Why couldn't she just leave me alone?

"Delrita, are you okay?" asked Avanelle.

"What? Oh, yeah. Just thinking about Heidi living in my house."

"It's hard, isn't it?" she said.

"It might be easier if she'd give me some space. I hate being hovered over all the time, and it's not natural for anyone to be that cheerful."

"Bottoms up," said Tree as he plunked our Cokes on the table. I scooted over to make room for him, but he didn't sit. He raised his drink to us, and headed over to the guys' booth.

I swallowed my disappointment and watched him go. He crowded in with the boys, and they all ogled Heidi and her friends, who were parading past them to claim the adjoining booth. Didn't those girls know that with all that weight on one side, the building might tip over?

"I forgot ketchup," chirped Heidi, and she sashayed past the boys again. Heads turned in unison to watch her, as if they were all pulled by the same string.

"Every time I see that girl, she's wearing something new," said Avanelle. "It's like she bought a whole wardrobe to make a fashion statement in Tangle Nook."

I didn't know how to respond to that. Heidi's Levi's, windbreaker, and Reeboks weren't all that different from what I wore, and yet Avanelle and I were best friends.

Avanelle leveled her green-eyed gaze across the restaurant. "I'm sick of hearing about Heidi's dad being on a secret military mission and her mom shooting photographs in Europe."

"She's trying to impress."

"Did you ever stop and think how unfair the world is?" asked Avanelle, dripping moisture from her straw onto the paper wrapper and watching it wriggle like a snake. "Girls like you and me, well, we've had our share of problems. Mom took care of all us kids by herself while Dad served his prison sentence. Here you are with no parents at all. And then there are golden girls like Heidi who wouldn't know a worry if they fell over it."

"Aunt Queenie says you and I've 'been through the fire.' That's supposed to mean troubles have made us stronger."

"Do you feel stronger?"

I heaved a sigh. "Not so you could tell it."

"Me, either. In fact, sometimes I feel limp as a dishrag." Avanelle grinned. "But you wouldn't know about that, since your hands never see dish water."

I grinned back. At first, I'd hated Aunt Queenie's fancy house with its dishwasher and vanilla-colored carpets and cold fireplace. I'd sought refuge in the Shacklefords' kitchen, where the dishes didn't match and there weren't enough chairs to go around. After standing up to eat a few times, I began to appreciate what I had with my aunt and uncle.

"Now that Dad's home, I've got even more dishes to wash," Avanelle said, but her eyes were shining and her freckles seemed to dance.

"And one less chair."

She giggled. "Speaking of furniture, I'm getting a vanity

dresser from Miss Myrtle as soon as I can figure out how to move it. She says the stool's too rickety for her old bones, and her eyes are so weak, she can't see in the mirror."

"That's great," I said, but I was sorry Avanelle had to settle for a hand-me-down dresser when my room was furnished with heirlooms.

At nine-fifteen on the dot, Aunt Queenie pulled up in her powder-blue Cadillac that was three years old, but looked brand-new.

"Here comes my ride," I said.

Avanelle took one last slurp through the straw and drained her Coke. "I'm right behind you."

As we scooted from the booth, we heard a burst of laughter from Tree's side of the room. Tree was fidgeting and reaching down the back of his shirt, and Heidi Grissom was just turning around in her seat. Obviously, she'd dropped ice down his back.

It's not fair, I thought. Heidi already has my house and my dad's antique shop, and now she's after Tree, too.

"That girl's a laugh a minute," said Avanelle.

"Yeah," I muttered, "and very immature."

Outside, Avanelle returned my jacket, waved at Aunt Queenie, and streaked across the lighted parking lot.

I opened the door and slid into the car, which smelled of lilacs and leather.

"How was the show?" asked Aunt Queenie.

"Fine."

She backed out of the parking space, eased us across the lot, and turned onto the street. "Did you have a good time at McDonald's?"

"It was okay."

"Well, I declare, Delrita, you were absolutely bubbly on the phone. What happened to make you lose your fizz?"

Lots of things. But I couldn't tell her that I felt sorry for the Shacklefords with their ancient station wagon and no way to get it fixed. For Joey Marcum, twenty-three years old and confined to a nursing home. For myself, because my parents were dead and Heidi Grissom was so cheerful I couldn't stand it. Aunt Queenie was used to handling problems at the crisis center, but these were beyond her reach.

Instead of answering her question, I asked one of my own. "Aunt Queenie, is there an age requirement in the Teen Buddies program?"

"Well, you do have to be a teenager."

"No, I mean for the residents. Could someone who's not old be a part of the program? Say someone who's only twenty-three?"

By the lights on the dashboard, I saw Aunt Queenie smile. "You're talking about Joey Marcum?"

"Yes. I'd like to be his buddy."

"I think that's a marvelous idea," she said, fingering the pencil in her hair. "You'd be perfect for him. You were excellent with Punky."

I narrowed my eyes and stared at her. Her touching that pencil was a dead giveaway. She'd *manipulated* me, sure as the world. I felt my face go hot with anger. "Aunt Queenie, you knew, didn't you, that I'd want to volunteer as soon as I met Joey?"

"Well, I declare, Delrita. Where'd you ever get an idea like that?"

"Let's just say you're not the only one who can figure all the angles."

"Angles?" she said. "I don't understand."

"You know that Joey and his mother are living at the nursing home. That I'm softhearted when it comes to handicapped people. That I've been wanting to see Outrageous on stage."

"Well, yes, but—"

"And *I* know that you're looking for teen volunteers. That you're not above lifting rocks, one at a time, to move a whole mountain. That you paid Outrageous out of your own pocket."

Her jaw tensed. "How'd you find out about the money?"

"Through the grapevine."

"Then there's a leak in the budget committee. That was supposed to be privileged information."

"Aunt Queenie, I don't care if you invite the whole Ringling Brothers Circus to the nursing home and pay for it yourself, but I wish you wouldn't meddle in my life."

"Meddle?" She yanked at the steering wheel when a tire dropped off the pavement. "Did you say 'meddle'?"

"Yes, I did, because my meeting Joey wasn't a coincidence, was it? It was a carefully plotted scheme."

"A *scheme?* How utterly selfish for you to suggest such a thing! I'll have you know, I had a lot of people in mind when I asked Tree to perform at the nursing home. The residents, the staff, even Tree himself. That boy needs every dime he can get!"

I had a sinking feeling in the pit of my stomach. Could I have been wrong about the pencil?

"I declare, Delrita. You've cut me to the core. My own niece, accusing me of plotting a scheme."

I didn't know what to do. If she were Mom, I could say I was sorry, and she would forgive and forget. But she was Queen Esther Holloway . . . and I was a misfit with both feet stuck in my mouth.

As if I didn't already feel bad enough, she said sarcastically, "Is this some fairy tale you've dreamed up? You're the poor, defenseless girl, and I'm the wicked stepmother?"

I leaned back against the soft leather seat and closed my eyes. No, not the wicked stepmother, just the distant queen.

7

Making Amends

Remorse made me sluggish as I changed into pajamas and brushed my teeth. I'd messed up royally with Aunt Queenie. I'd pushed her way too hard with that smart-aleck line about the carefully plotted scheme.

Since she'd had time to cool off, maybe I could set things right. Make amends, as Dad used to say.

I found her in the family room, ready for bed in her blue satin robe and matching slippers, her face shiny from moisturizing lotion. She was crocheting up a storm and watching the news with her father and Uncle Bert.

"I'm going to bed now," I said. Another great line. Tornadoes are on a rampage in the Midwest, and Delrita Jensen is calling it a day.

My aunt and uncle told me good night, while Mr. Roebuck grunted in my direction.

"Aunt Queenie, I—uh—want to apologize for what I said in the car."

"Apology accepted," she replied curtly, "but I do hope you'll remember that the sun doesn't rise and set around you."

I slunk back to my room and lay stiff as a plank in my bed. Every time I closed my eyes, I saw myself as a drain, sucking away the time she'd rather spend on important volunteer projects. I was afraid that in her list of priorities, I was way down at the bottom of the pile.

In my sleep, I plodded around the track at Special Olympics, trying to catch up with the dozen runners ahead of me. All were athletes with disabilities, but they were flying with the wind. In my hand was a vial of nitroglycerin pills. If a runner had a heart attack, I would slip one of the tiny white pills under his tongue.

"Wait! Slow down!" I hollered, but no one listened. The hot asphalt was melting licorice, clinging to my feet, and I could only shuffle along.

Cheering on the sidelines was a perfect row of huggers, the tall ones on the left and the short ones on the right. Chief of the huggers was Aunt Queenie in her jeans and sweatshirt and grungy tennis shoes, her long hair blowing in the breeze.

As Punky and Joey crossed the finish line, Aunt Queenie sprinted forward to meet them. "Good job!" she yelled, throwing her arms around their sweaty bodies in a three-way hug.

When a female runner crossed the line, she yelled, "Good job!" and hugged her, too. . . .

I woke up tired, as though I'd been fighting that licorice

asphalt for real. The room was dark and smelled like wax. The heating vent was making Punky's crayons potent.

Without switching on a light, I threw back the covers and stumbled in to use the john. I sat there thinking about the Aunt Queenie in my dream. She did exist—but only on Saturdays, and only at Special Olympics. Who'd have guessed that such a prissy lady would get so close to people dripping sweat?

There it was. Another contradiction, another paradox, staring me in the face.

With a sigh, I flushed the stool and went back to my room. It was five o'clock, straight up. I turned on the radio, intending to climb back into bed, but "The Star-Spangled Banner" was playing.

The song spun me into a whirlpool of memory, and I saw Punky saluting Old Glory at the post office. I saw him plucking off his cowboy hat at the start of a parade. I heard him ordering, "Up, dummy!" to a man sprawled on the curb during the passing of the flag.

"Up, dummy," I whispered, and in this dark room all by myself, I stayed on my feet for the national anthem.

When the deejay's wake-up greeting came on the air, my armpits were damp, and my silky pajamas felt clammy and cold against my skin. Knowing I wouldn't be able to go back to sleep, I turned on the light. The clowns I'd carved for Punky stood on the dresser like silent sentinels.

As always, when the past closed in on me, I felt a powerful urge to carve. I could find comfort in the smell of new basswood, the feel of it in my hands, the sense of control that carving gave me.

At my desk, I positioned the bath towel in front of me and removed the swan from the Barbie case. Using my smallest V-tool, I began etching feathers on a delicate wing.

Slowly, my tension ebbed away, and I let my thoughts run free. This swan reminded me of Herkimer, the first swan I'd carved with outstretched wings. "Pretty bird," Punky called it, and he'd given it to Susie, one of his friends at the sheltered workshop.

I pictured Joey Marcum at the workshop. Pictured him buying red cowboy boots with his first paycheck.

Maybe I should carve a bear for him, but not just any bear—a teddy bear, a replica of Peanut.

"Somethin' wrong, girlie?"

"Oh!" I jumped, gouging my palm with the V-tool and snapping off the swan's wing. It skittered across the desk and landed in the doorway at Orvis Roebuck's feet.

"Didn't mean to scare you," he said. "Saw a light under your door and thought maybe you was sick or something."

I was sick, all right. Sick that my beautiful swan was broken. Sick at all those hours wasted. A bitter taste and a bitter retort rose in my throat, but I swallowed both. "I'm okay," I mumbled. "Just couldn't sleep."

Mr. Roebuck picked up the wing and handed it to me. "Looks like you broke off a piece. Maybe you can glue it back on."

Glue? Did the sculptor glue arms on the Venus de Milo? Did Michelangelo paste pictures in the Sistine Chapel? "No, it's junk now," I said, flinging the wing and the swan into the wastebasket.

"Perfection, is it? So Queen's rubbing off on you." Mr. Roebuck backed out the door and disappeared.

What a way to start the day. I wiped a spot of blood off my palm with a tissue, then stood over the wastebasket and brushed wood shavings off my pajamas.

I needed a shower, so I dug for clean clothes. Naturally, my green GOTTA BE ME T-shirt was still in the dryer with the other shirts I'd forgotten to fold.

I headed for the laundry room, and there was Aunt Queenie, emptying the trash can into a big plastic bag. She was still wearing the toilet paper turban that protected her hairdo at night. "Good morning," she said brightly as I sauntered in.

Relief swept through me. I was forgiven. "Hi," I said, flashing a megaton smile.

Aunt Queenie finished with the wastebasket and hustled off—a germ warrior in a satin robe and toilet paper. Definitely a paradox.

Grinning, I turned on the dryer to fluff my shirts. Two minutes later, hot shirts in my arms, I saw Mr. Roebuck coming out of my room. I froze. What possible business could he have there? Another apology for the swan? Too late. He'd already blown it by invading my space without permission.

I hurried to my room and locked the door behind me. Nothing seemed out of place, but I felt uneasy as I laid aside the shirt I wanted and hung the others in the closet.

Then I found this note lying on the desk: "Sorry about the swan. Orvis Roebuck."

I crumpled the paper and tossed it into the trash basket.

The broken swan was already gone. The germ warrior had struck again.

I was stepping out of the shower when a news bulletin came on the radio: "A woman in Tangle Nook awakened last night to the sound of someone breaking into her house. She hid in the closet and called the police on her cordless phone. When the squad car arrived, the intruder had already gone, taking with him a diamond ring, an antique clock, and fifty-six dollars in cash. Police Chief Robert Nichols said this is the third such burglary reported in Tangle Nook in the past ten days. . . ."

Feeling cold and exposed, I dressed hurriedly. Knowing Mr. Roebuck had been in my room was bad enough. How horrifying it would be to wake up and find a thief in the house.

After blow-drying my hair, I pulled up the sides and fastened them at my crown with an ivy-patterned barrette. The new style gave me an intriguing look. I hoped Tree would notice.

In the kitchen, I found Uncle Bert and Aunt Queenie drinking coffee at the table, and I paused in the doorway to study them. Now that I knew there was fifteen years' difference between them, I couldn't decide whether Uncle Bert had aged early or Aunt Queenie was well preserved.

A slight paunch was showing above the waistband of his gray slacks, and his bald head gleamed in the sunlight. He'd rolled up his shirtsleeves and slung his tie over his shoulder because of his tendency to spill things.

Without all that toilet paper, Aunt Queenie appeared

younger than he did. Nice figure. Lacy white blouse and purple skirt. Lavender eye shadow. Purple pencil and purple shoes.

"I declare, Bert," she said, "I know I'd just die of fright if I woke up and heard someone prowling through the house."

"Your dad does it all the time. At three o'clock this morning, he—"

"What's the holdup?" asked Mr. Roebuck behind me. "Are they charging admission?"

I gritted my teeth and moved on into the kitchen.

"Morning, everybody," said Uncle Bert.

"Morning." I kissed his pate, like Punky used to do, and took my seat.

After the blessing, Uncle Bert said, "I like your new hairstyle, Delrita. So straight and natural. Most girls these days want frizzle and kinks."

"Avanelle hates hers," I said as I drizzled skim milk over my cereal and strawberries. "Says she looks like a Chore-Boy."

"Well, I declare," said Aunt Queenie. "Hair and scouring pads. Let's not discuss such things at the breakfast table. What I would like to discuss is whether you're serious about being a Teen Buddy to Joey Marcum."

"I'm serious."

"I think working with Joey will help your healing process," she said, "but just remember, Joey isn't Punky, and you can never bring Punky back."

"I know."

As she studied my face, I saw an unmistakable sadness in

hers. I remembered her tears the night Santa, in person, came to this house to deliver the presents she'd bought and wrapped for Punky.

At times like this, I truly loved Aunt Queenie.

And then she ruined it by saying, "Just keep in mind that if you take this on, you can't be backing out."

"I'm not a quitter."

"I didn't say you were. But understand that you'll be expected to visit Joey at least once a week. Be his friend. Entertain him in some way. It'll be difficult to communicate with him, because of his speech defect."

"I can handle it," I said crossly. I might not know what Joey was saying in words, but I could read his face, his mannerisms, his eyes.

"I suggest you try a practice visit. See how it goes before you make the commitment."

"She told you she can handle it," said Mr. Roebuck. "What do you want her to do? Sign in blood on the dotted line?"

Here we go again, I thought. Another mealtime. Another war.

But Aunt Queenie let it go. She pursed her lips and smeared low-fat margarine on a piece of toast.

I said to Uncle Bert, "Joey's got a teddy bear named Peanut, and I want to carve a bear for him just like it. If I draw the pattern, would you cut some carving blanks?"

"Not me. I'm scared to death of machinery. Clumsy, too. I might cut off something I'll need later."

"Any fool oughta be able to handle a band saw," said Mr. Roebuck.

We all gaped at him. He was grinning—a lopsided grin because of that scar on his cheek—and he added, "So I reckon I could give it a try."

You could have scraped Aunt Queenie's eyeballs off her face with a spoon. "You, Pop?" she said.

"Yes, me, Queen. And don't give me that look like I've got two heads."

"But Pop, your hands are so shaky."

"Queen, give me some credit here. You pestered me until I volunteered to help with crafts up there at the nursing home. I've done tin-punching. I've used electric scissors to cut out rag dolls. Don't tell me I can't run a band saw. I can and I will to help the girlie here."

I winced at the "girlie," but at least I was going to have my carving blanks.

The old man turned his piercing blue eyes on me. "Let me tell you a little story about Peanut. Joey lost him last week, and next thing anybody knew, the paramedics were at the door."

"The paramedics?" I said.

"Yep. Joey and his mother were visiting at her niece's house, and Joey got real upset when he couldn't find his bear. He slipped into the kitchen and called nine-one-one."

I giggled—at the story and at Uncle Bert's reaction to it. He snorted into his coffee and dribbled some on his shirt. "He didn't!"

"He certainly did," said Aunt Queenie.

Uncle Bert stared at her. "But that's for emergencies."

A smile was tugging at the corners of her mouth. "And losing that bear *is* an emergency to Joey. He has quite a few emergencies, and the paramedics play along with him."

"Queen," growled her father, "this is my story, so let me tell it."

With a sweep of her hand, she gave him the floor.

Mr. Roebuck turned back to me and folded his arms on the table. "Every time Joey loses his bear or gets scolded by his mother, he calls the paramedics and they settle him down over the phone. No harm done. Only reason there was a problem last week was because the new dispatcher didn't know the situation and couldn't understand what Joey was saying, so she sent the ambulance to the address showing up on the board."

"Let me guess," said Uncle Bert. "The paramedics saved the day."

Mr. Roebuck cackled. "They found Peanut in the nursing home's van and delivered him to Joey at the niece's house. The little critter was strapped to a stretcher and wearing an oxygen mask."

When I gave my rough sketch of a teddy bear to Mr. Roebuck, he folded it in half and stuck it in his pocket.

"I appreciate—" I said, but he cut me off.

"Just making amends for scaring you this morning. Now get on off to school."

Making amends. Somehow that phrase didn't have the same ring to it, coming from him.

He'd said any fool ought to be able to operate a band saw. I hoped he was right. I'd never hear the end of it if he whacked off a finger.

8

The Shacklefords

It had rained in the night, and the air smelled of wet earth. As I walked to Avanelle's house, I took in the sounds of other peoples' lives—a hammer banging in the distance, cars starting, doors slamming, moms yelling last-minute instructions. Somebody somewhere was frying bacon, and the aroma made me sad. I missed Mom's bacon-and-egg breakfasts, almost as much as I missed Dad's chili. "Blue flame," he called it, because the jalapeño peppers would set you on fire.

"Hi, Velveeta. Didn't you see me wavin'?"

I looked up blankly. My feet had carried me to the Shacklefords' house, where four-year-old Birdie sat astraddle the front porch rail. The hammering I'd heard was coming from the backyard.

"Velveeta?" Birdie said.

Her expression, so intense, put me in mind of a very wise, very freckled pixie. Her pink pajama shirt was buttoned crooked, and the sunshine seemed to set fire to her tangled curls. I smiled when I saw she was wearing scuffed cowboy boots. They were Randolph's, and he'd have a fit if he found them on his little sister's feet. "Sorry, Birdie," I said as I climbed the steps. "I didn't see you. I was thinking."

"Prob'ly somethin' wrong with your eyes," she said. *"I* can see and think at the same time. My dad can, too, else he'd hit his thumb with the hammer. He's fixin' the porch for his privates."

She meant "privacy," and it was all I could do to keep a straight face.

With a question in her eyes, she studied the letters on my shirt.

" 'Gotta . . . be . . . me,' " I read, pointing at each word.

" 'Gotta be me'?" she echoed as one of her boots slid off and thunked onto the porch. "That's silly. Who else would you be?"

I tousled her hair. "Nobody. I just gotta be me—Delrita-Velveeta Jensen."

Laughing, she hopped off the rail, rammed her bare foot back into the boot, and pulled me into the house.

The noise level would have shot a decibel reading right off the scale. The hammering from out back. Gordy dumping a box of scrap wood blocks onto the coffee table. Eddie ka-blamming with a curtain rod rifle. Randolph muttering and belly flopping as he felt under the couch for his cowboy boots. I could see Mrs. Shackleford in the kitchen holding a spoon, and I heard a jumble of words and squeals, so I assumed she was urging Ellie to open wide.

Tree, I knew, would already have left for school. I didn't

see Avanelle, but through the doorway that led to the girls' bedroom, I spotted her purse and books on the cardboard box that served as a bedside table. I hoped she'd figure out a way to move Miss Myrtle's dresser soon.

"Velveeta's here," Birdie announced over the clamor.

Nobody heard.

Determined to be noticed, Birdie pulled me to the kitchen. Ellie saw us coming and gurgled happily, spewing oatmeal at her mom.

The phrase "spitting image" popped into my mind. All these redheaded kids were the spitting image of Mrs. Shackleford, except they didn't have the worry lines around their emerald eyes.

"Velveeta's here," said Birdie.

"So I see." Gardenia Shackleford smiled at me and swabbed at the oatmeal in her hair. "Things are hectic this morning."

"Nothing new about that," I said, and pointed out a spot she'd missed on her flannel nightgown.

The usual aroma of oatmeal and cinnamon hung in the air, but the light that normally streamed in from the back porch had been cut off by a sheet of paneling. I caught a glimpse of Mr. Shackleford, walking across the porch with a hammer in his hand. His dark hair, slightly damp, was slicked back in a sixties style. He was wearing jeans and a chambray shirt with a missing button that showed a "V" of hairy chest. When he reversed direction, he saw me and waved. "Hi, Delrita."

"Hi. Looks like you're hard at work."

"I'm trying. Mama's a real slave-driver," he said with a teasing grin at his wife.

I chuckled. I'd been afraid of him when I met him—a man fresh out of prison, his brown eyes haunted, his skin pale, and his body built up from lifting weights. He'd spoken too loud, laughed too loud, and he'd seemed bigger than life. He wasn't like that now. Three weeks of freedom had added color to his face and gentleness to his voice. Not finding a job had deepened the haunted look in his eyes.

"If there's any slave-driving going on here, Trezane's doing it to himself," said Mrs. Shackleford, spooning another bite of cereal into Ellie's mouth. "He's tired of us having to sleep on the floor."

She watched as Randolph, clad in faded jeans and a T-shirt damp around the neck, stomped barefooted through the kitchen into the bathroom, then back into the living room.

"Randolph's mad at the world this morning," she said. "I made him wash his hair, he can't find his boots, and Tree went off to school without him."

Using only my eyes, I called her attention to Birdie's feet.

Mrs. Shackleford saw the boots, and the lines around her eyes crinkled as she smiled. "Quick, Birdie," she whispered, "take those off and hide them out there with your dad. He hasn't searched there yet."

When Birdie obeyed, her mother said, "She's so precocious. Half the time, I find myself outdistanced by an almost-five-year-old."

"Hi, Delrita," said Avanelle, entering the kitchen. Her

jeans and blue button-down shirt were well-worn, but they had the warm, fresh smell of having been recently ironed. I felt a twinge of guilt about the clothes I'd fluffed in the dryer.

"Randolph's an old silly," said Birdie, emerging from the porch. She giggled and wiggled her toes. "His boots were right here on my feet, and he couldn't even see 'em."

"Why didn't you tell him where they were?" asked Avanelle.

"Because he'd have made me give 'em back." Birdie tapped her head and shot me a mischievous grin. "*I* can see and think at the same time."

Randolph was still in a bad mood when we left for school, and he ran ahead of Avanelle and me.

"Randolph, wait up," Avanelle called. "Watch that street."

He slowed his steps, looked both ways, and crossed the street by himself.

"The little stinker," his sister said. "He never listens to me."

Not for the first time, I wondered about the gap in the Shackleford kids' ages. Randolph, at seven, was the third oldest child. It seemed strange to me that Mrs. Shackleford would give birth to Tree and Avanelle within a year of each other, then wait seven years before having five more kids with hardly a break in between.

We hurried along behind Randolph to make sure he reached the elementary school, then cut across the back way to the junior high. As usual, ninth-graders had staked out their territory on the low brick wall behind the building. From a distance, one student in a red, white, and blue windbreaker stood out like an American flag.

"Up, dummy," I murmured.

"I was thinking the same thing," said Avanelle. "Maybe we ought to salute."

Laughing, we did salute, but our good humor faded when we got close enough to see that the person in the patriotic jacket was Heidi Grissom.

"That girl's got more new clothes than J.C. Penney," said Avanelle.

I didn't care about that. I cared about Heidi being perched next to Tree on the wall.

Tree wasn't handsome, really, but the sight of him always shifted my heart into high gear. His muscular body filled out every inch of his Tangle Nook Wildcats football jersey and jeans. In the sunlight, Heidi's cloud of golden curls floated disgustingly close to his moptop.

"I don't know how he does it," said Avanelle.

"Does what?"

"Gets you girls all googly-eyed. He tells me I'm adopted because I'm such a wart. Hid my bra this morning when we disagreed over the clowning money. Believe me, you wouldn't like him half as much if you had to live with him."

Uproarious laughter from the wall. Tree was evidently tickled to death at something Heidi said.

I wanted to kick myself from here to St. Louis for having straight, mousy-brown hair.

9

The History Assignment

In English first hour, all I could think about was Tree and Heidi, Heidi and Tree. In second hour study hall, the geometric figures in my math book looked like hieroglyphics on a cave wall.

When third hour rolled around, I hurried next door to art class, because Mr. Casey allowed free-form seating. I grabbed a table for myself and Avanelle, who had to come from history class at the far end of the hall.

She stalked in and plopped down in a chair. "The teachers in this school are in cahoots," she said. "You won't *believe* what Mrs. Bagby's cooked up for the whole eighth grade."

"Something tells me it isn't brownies."

"I wish," said Avanelle. "You know how the English teachers had us practicing interviews? Well, now I know why. It was to get us ready for our next *history* assignment."

"Which is?"

"Interviewing a combat veteran. Mrs. Bagby gave us questions to ask if we need help getting started." Avanelle pulled a paper from her pocket, unfolded it, and read: " 'Did you enlist, or were you drafted? Where did you see combat? Were you wounded?' All kinds of stuff like that."

I thought about Joseph Cable, our neighbor across the street who'd lost an arm in Korea. He was a friendly guy. I wouldn't mind interviewing him.

"You want to see this?" asked Avanelle, offering me the list.

"No, thanks. I'll get my own sixth hour."

She shrugged. "Whatever. Uh-oh. Here comes Miss America."

I frowned at Heidi Grissom, breezing into class. She'd shed the patriotic windbreaker, but she was still decked out like a flag. Red T-shirt with "USA" emblazoned on the front, stylishly faded blue jeans, blue-starred laces in white Reeboks. I love America—feel a thrill at the Pledge of Allegiance—but I couldn't stand those clothes. Heidi would have taken them from *my* closet at *my* house.

She scanned the room, deciding where to park her bod. Oh, no. She was heading our way.

"Hi, guys!" she said, taking a seat at our table and suffocating me with the scent of musk cologne.

"Hi." Avanelle and I sounded like good little girls, being polite, but the look that passed between us said otherwise.

"Wish I'd brought the postcard Mother sent me from France," Heidi said. "It shows the cutest little boy driving an oxcart. She's working her way toward Paris. My next postcard will probably be the Eiffel Tower."

Avanelle and I kicked each other under the table. Brag, brag, brag.

"These photographs she's taking," Avanelle said. "What're they for?"

"Mother's a freelancer. She markets her work when it's done."

Avanelle squinted at Heidi. "Don't you miss her something terrible, especially since your dad's on that secret mission?"

"Well, sure, but she has her career to think about. Besides," Heidi said, examining a blood-red fingernail, "Nana and Gramps are great. They've got plenty of time for me since they sold the supermarket in Little Rock."

"Supermarket?" I yelped. "You mean they didn't run an antique shop?"

"Oh, no. Gramps doesn't even know antiques that well. He bought the shop here so he'd have something to dabble with. Says he's too young for a rocking chair, unless it's an old one he can sell."

I was steaming. Talk about the straw that broke the camel's back. Gramps Naramore was *dabbling* in the antique business Dad had worked so hard starting up last year.

The bell rang, and Mr. Casey handed out our watercolor paintings. "I want these finished today," he said, "so use this hour to fix whatever problems you might have."

"An hour to fix this mess," groaned Avanelle, who didn't have much of an eye for art. My efforts to teach her to carve had been a total flop.

Heidi chattered about her mother's escapades in France

as we worked, as though Avanelle and I were her oldest friends.

Fat chance. I would never be friends with Heidi. I would never set foot in her house.

Still, my gaze kept wandering toward her painting of a woman peering at the sky. She'd used sepia tones to capture the folds of the shirt, the squint of the eyes, the creases in the face. That surprised me. You expected someone as flamboyant as Heidi to go for the gaudy colors.

Heidi didn't notice I'd been giving her the cold shoulder. As I stood back to examine my painting of a dogwood tree, she said, "Delrita, that's terrific. You're probably the only real artist in this room."

"I wouldn't say that," I mumbled. "It's just a tree."

"But you're a woodcarver, too."

Avanelle drew in her breath sharply. She knew how close-mouthed I was about my carving.

"I—who—who told you that?" I stammered.

"Some woman named Grotzinger who has a retarded daughter. They came into Gramps's shop last week just to look around. Susie, the daughter, had a bunch of things in a cigar box, and one of them was a swan you carved."

Herkimer. Punky's "pretty bird" gift to Susie.

"Gramps was really nervous because of this one cabinet Susie wouldn't leave alone. It was rare and *very* expensive, according to his guidebook. It had fancy scrollwork at the top and curved glass doors."

Mom's china cabinet. Her favorite antique. My stomach roiled, and I felt scalding tears behind my eyes.

"Look, Heidi," said Avanelle with a worried glance at me, "Delrita doesn't make a big deal about her woodcarving, so let's not talk about it."

I wanted to shout, It's not the carving! It's the *cabinet!* But I didn't dare open my mouth. If I did, I'd lose control. I'd curl up into a blubbering ball of misery.

Good-time Heidi didn't even notice. She went right on talking about how Susie had set the swan behind the glass, pretending it was a pretty bird on TV.

I said nothing, but I was gripping the table so hard my fingers hurt.

"Heidi, please," said Avanelle. "Just drop it."

Heidi stared at me. "What's the big deal? If I could carve like you do, I'd want the world to know."

When I still didn't reply, she took up the slack. "Well, anyway, that swan of Susie's is neat. I've been wondering if I could do woodcarving myself." Suddenly, her eyes lit up, and she said, "Hey, Delrita, maybe you could give me some pointers. I'd—"

"No!"

Heidi jerked back in her chair. She glanced from me to Avanelle, as if to say, What's with you two? Her blue eyes registered puzzlement and hurt.

But at least she stopped talking.

We went back to work on our paintings, and with each stroke of my brush, I felt my tension ebbing. I grudgingly admitted to myself that Heidi couldn't know about my mother's china cabinet. Even Avanelle didn't know. How could I talk valuable antiques to a girl whose bedside table was a cardboard box?

Another thought niggled at the back of my mind: It was my own fault that Mom's cabinet was up for grabs. I'd told Uncle Bert I never wanted to see it again.

In PE class, we counted off in fours to make up teams for volleyball. When I was on the court, I kept my eyes on the ball. When I was on the bench, I kept my eyes on Heidi, whose team was playing Avanelle's.

Her interest in woodcarving gnawed away at me. Time and again, she set up the ball at the net, so one of her teammates could spike it. She had long, capable fingers—fingers that had captured the creases in a woman's face. Fingers that, with practice, could make something beautiful with a knife and a hunk of wood. . . .

I jumped at the ten-minute bell, just like I'd jumped at Mr. Roebuck's voice this morning. Discarding thoughts of Heidi, as if she were the broken swan, I joined my classmates heading for the locker room.

Centered on the blackboard behind our history teacher's desk was a front page from *The Kansas City Star,* with her picture and big bold headlines that read:

CORA MAE BAGBY
GOSSIP COLUMNIST FOR THE PAST
MAKES HISTORY COME ALIVE
FOR DEADHEAD STUDENTS

Mrs. Bagby had told us the page was a dummy, a gag gift from a former student. Still, those fake headlines spoke the truth. You could count on her to dig out little-known facts about historical characters and events. For instance, she'd said Abraham Lincoln's gauntness was probably due to Marfan syndrome, a disorder that affects blood circulation and causes abnormally long bones in the arms and legs.

As soon as the tardy bell rang, Mrs. Bagby stood up from her desk and eyed the class. We all but snapped to attention in our seats. She was short and squat like an army tank, and when she fired information, it was usually something you wanted to hear.

She marched back and forth across the room, talking about specific battles of World War Two. After a while, she stopped marching and ran a hand through her grizzled hair. "You can read about the battles in your textbooks," she said, "but I want you to understand the human side of war—the suffering, the homesickness, the deprivation. Most of all, I want you to understand about love of country, which is why men leave their homes and families to fight and die on foreign soil."

No one moved. Mrs. Bagby was leading up to a particular incident. We knew it when she rested her rump on her desk.

With tears in her eyes, she told us a story about an infantryman who was nearly cut in half by a Japanese mortar shell on Guadalcanal.

"His buddies could do nothing except prop him against a tree and wait for him to die," she said. "Several times, he tried to speak, but he couldn't make himself be understood. Finally, the commanding officer put his ear right up to the infantryman's mouth and listened closely to the message. What he wanted was to see the American flag. When the officer brought the flag, a look of peace came over the infantryman's face. He said clearly, 'Something to die for,' and closed his eyes in death."

The story gave me goosebumps. A hasty glance at my classmates' somber faces told me they'd been as touched by the story as I.

Mrs. Bagby's eyes glistened as she surveyed us. "As I hoped, that story has made an impression on you," she said. "There are many moving stories of war that have never been printed in the history books. They're in the memories of the men who fought the battles and felt the fear. That's why I want each of you to interview a combat veteran of World War Two—"

Crud. She'd shot down my plan to interview Mr. Cable, and the only World War Two veteran I knew was Orvis Roebuck. Interviewing him was out of the question. This morning was the first time he'd said a civilized word to me in two whole weeks. And last night, when Aunt Queenie brought up his military service, he'd told her flat out that he didn't want to talk about it.

My classmates were buzzing like a swarm of confused bees, asking questions about the assignment.

"Quiet!" ordered Mrs. Bagby. "Everybody quiet!"

The kids fell silent, but Roger McPherson waved his arm wildly.

"Yes, Roger?" the teacher said.

"My dad was a Green Beret who fought the communists in Vietnam. Why can't I interview him?"

Addressing the whole class, Mrs. Bagby said sadly, "The Vietnam War was your parents' war, a war with different tactics, different weapons, different attitudes. Many Americans opposed the war in Vietnam, and some men even fled to Canada to escape the draft. Returning soldiers did not receive a heroes' welcome, but were often treated with contempt."

"Why?" asked Greg Moritz.

"Ignorance. Small-mindedness." Then the teacher's face brightened, and she said, "But World War Two was a time when Americans pulled together, when an air of unity pervaded this great land of ours. People were proud to be citizens of a nation fighting to end oppression. Young men were eager to enlist, to fight for democracy."

Mrs. Bagby moved up and down the aisles, handing out the interview questions. "If you need these guidelines, use them," she said. "If you don't, throw them away. They're mainly to help trigger the memories of the veterans. These men will be in their seventies, and some of them may be a little foggy on the details. Some will be reluctant to talk about the war, but others will be glad for a new ear to listen to their stories."

"How do we find these guys?" asked Greg.

"They're all around you. Ryan's great-uncle was a paratrooper. Mr. Leeson at Commercial Bank was a bombadier on a Flying Fortress. Ask your family, your neighbors, your friends at church. Or call the VFW—that's Veterans of Foreign Wars—for information."

VFW. The pressure was off. I'd forgotten about that nice old man who helped out at the sheltered workshop. I'd seen him wearing his VFW cap at a parade, and I thought of him as "the general." When Punky was dying at Christmastime, the general had visited him in a Santa Claus suit.

"You'll have two weeks to conduct your interview and write your report," Mrs. Bagby said.

"How long does it have to be?" asked Roger.

"That depends on your veteran. One man's story may fill three pages, while another may fill thirty."

"Thirty pages!" we chorused.

Mrs. Bagby gave us a wise, commander-in-chief smile. "I think you'll be pleasantly surprised by this assignment. The words will practically write themselves. Oh, here's one more thing. Although the other eighth-grade classes have the same assignment, you'll get extra credit if you interview a person whom no one else has chosen. The object of that is to inspire each student to do his own work."

The bell rang. I sailed from the room, dodging classmates who were still swarming, still confused.

I was at my locker, swapping my history book for science, when someone tapped me on the shoulder and said, "Mrs. Bagby really laid it on us, didn't she?" It was Heidi, who had history fifth hour.

"Yeah," I grunted without turning around.

"My father knows a lot of retired colonels, but since he's on that secret mission, I'll have to find my own vet. Have you thought of anybody yet?"

I shrugged and slammed my locker. I refused to tell her about the general. For all I knew, he'd been a private first class.

Heidi picked at a fingernail for a few seconds. Then she

looked me in the eye and said, "Delrita, can I ask you a question?"

"Fire away."

"What's the matter? What have I done? Why are you mad at me?"

"That's three questions, and it's time for the bell. I've got to get to science." I turned on my heel and walked away. Get a clue, Heidi, I seethed. My house, my antique shop, even my *closet,* for crying out loud.

A little voice said I was being unfair, but I didn't care. Life itself was unfair.

The last class of the day didn't improve my disposition. I looked at various types of fungi—molds, mildews, mushrooms, rusts, and smuts. I learned that all fungi are parasites that live off other organisms. They don't have their own roots.

That was a downer, since I felt pretty rootless myself.

10

The Enemy

Avanelle was waiting for me at my locker, her eyes flashing like green sparks. "He's doing it again," she fumed.

I didn't even have to ask. She meant that Tree was staying late to help Coach Winslow, and she'd have to walk Randolph home.

"Why does he always pick Wednesdays?" she groused. "He knows I have to sit with Miss Myrtle."

"I'll see that Randolph gets home."

"Yeah, I know. It just burns me up that Tree takes me for granted."

We joined the tide of students flowing from the school, and as we cut across to the elementary, Avanelle said, "Did you know Miss Myrtle was in the Red Cross during the war?"

"No. We've never really talked much—just 'hi' and 'bye' at church."

"She was activity director for the wounded at hospitals overseas. When the war was almost over, she was sent to Burma where American forces were building that big road."

"The Burma Road. I saw it in a movie."

"There were tigers, headhunters, and kraits—deadly poisonous snakes—but Miss Myrtle lived in a thatch house with mosquito nets for windows. She even rode an elephant once."

"That's hard to imagine. She's so frail and sickly now."

"I know, but this afternoon in study hall, it hit me that she'd be a good person to interview for the history assignment."

I glanced sideways at her. If she was teasing, she was doing it with a straight face. "Women didn't fight in the war," I said, "so they don't qualify as combat veterans."

"But they served in other ways. I checked with Mrs. Bagby, and she gave me the okay. Says it'll be interesting to hear about the war from a female's point of view. How about you? I guess you'll interview Mr. Roebuck?"

"No, I'm going after the general."

"He doesn't live here anymore. I think he moved to Florida. Why not just settle for Mr. Roebuck? He's right there under your nose."

"One, he doesn't like me very much. Two, I haven't found anybody he does like, except for Joey Marcum. Three, with nearly five thousand people in Tangle Nook, I can surely find a veteran who doesn't chew tobacco and gob on the—"

"Hey, guess what!" said Randolph, running up between us. "Elmer's a girl, and she's got a nest of babies."

"Who's Elmer?" I asked.

Randolph giggled. "A white rat. The babies don't have hair, so they look like little pink thumbs."

Avanelle and I laughed at his description. Then she headed off to Miss Myrtle's, and I walked Randolph home.

Birdie, Eddie, and Gordy were up to their usual tricks—digging holes in the yard with spoons. Ellie was eating dirt.

"Hey, Velveeta," called Birdie, "come and see what we're doin'."

I walked over and bragged on the new holes.

The screen door popped open, and Mrs. Shackleford stepped onto the porch. "Hi, Delrita. Come on in and have a cupcake."

"Yay! Cupcakes!" yelled her kids.

I scooped up Ellie, sat her on my hip, and clambered into the house with the mob.

Aunt Queenie's car wasn't in the garage, because this was her day to work until five at the crisis center. I entered the house quietly, hoping I could slip into my room without Orvis Roebuck knowing I was home.

Clutching my books to my chest, I stood in the kitchen and listened. I could hear the grandfather clock ticking. The water softener cycling. Cubes falling from the ice maker. The old man talking.

When I heard the word "Nazis," I knew he was talking about the war.

I tiptoed to the door and peeked into the family room. His lounge chair was angled away from me, so I could see only the lower part of him—fatigue pants, slippers propped up on the foot rest, and a tape recorder in his lap.

". . . on his body," he was saying. "So much blood. For three days, they kept me on the mattress with the dead man."

I gasped.

"What the—?" spouted Mr. Roebuck, slamming the foot rest to the floor. He heaved sideways in the chair and glared at me with eyes that were red and mean. The puckered scar was a white bull's-eye in his liver-colored face.

Did he think I was the enemy? Had recalling three days with a dead man warped his sense of time and place?

Mr. Roebuck flung the recorder onto the end table, and used both hands to push himself from the chair. He stumbled toward me, his expression dazed.

I backed away from the door and fled down the hall to my room.

"Wait!" he ordered.

I didn't wait. I slammed and locked my door, then leaned against it. If he was off his rocker . . . If he thought I was the enemy . . . Moments later, a knock hammered against my head, and I jumped.

"Open up!" said Mr. Roebuck. When I didn't answer, he barked, "Are you gonna open this door, or not?"

Not.

"Say something, girlie. Answer me."

Girlie? For the first time ever, I was glad to hear that word. It meant he knew I wasn't a Nazi.

"I'm not gonna hurt you. I wouldn't hurt you or anybody else."

Still apprehensive, I tossed my books onto the desk.

That's when I saw the carving blanks. Four little lumps of basswood, basically shaped like teddy bears.

"I'm sorry if I scared you, but you walked in on me at a bad time. The truth is, *you* scared *me*. You caught me reliving some horrible things about the war."

I glanced at the carving blanks again. Four teddy bears cut to my specifications. Hoping I wouldn't regret it, I slowly opened the door.

Mr. Roebuck's eyes were red-rimmed, but they no longer looked mean. "Thanks, girlie," he said. "Now you and me need to talk about that tape recorder. You can't breathe a word about it."

"Why not?"

He pulled a red handkerchief from his pants pocket and wiped his face. "I'm testing myself, to see if I can call up— uh—certain things—without going to pieces. A man has his pride. He doesn't want his buddies to see him bawling like a baby."

Baffled, I could only stare at him.

"You see, girlie, the outfit I served with in France is having a reunion in Kansas City. In June. To commemorate D-Day. For three days, they'll talk about nothing but the war. I've kept some terrible memories buried all these years, and I'm not sure I want to dig 'em all up. Especially in front of a crowd."

"So what's the secret about the tape recorder?"

"You know how Queen is. Once she gets hold of something, she won't let it go. She doesn't know about the reunion, and I plan to keep it that way. Don't want her pestering me to attend."

I nodded. Aunt Queenie could pester. No doubt about that.

"No way in thunder will I go to Kansas City if I can't even tell this story to myself. But that's not the worst of it. This morning, Queen came up with the harebrained idea that I should write a book about my career in the army, to give me something to do." He snorted. "A *book!* You'd think I was General Patton, old 'Blood and Guts' himself."

I stared at the tattoos on his forearms and the tobacco dribbles on his chin. Who'd ever want to read a book he'd write?

"Queen says for me to record everything on tape, and she'll take it from there—typing, editing, and I don't know what all. If she finds out what I'm doing, she'll pester me to death. She'll want the tapes, so she can start on that book."

I could see it now—Aunt Queenie listening, typing, organizing.

Mr. Roebuck gave me a sly smile. "I'd never have thought of the recorder, if she hadn't mentioned it. I went out and bought it this morning as soon as she left the house. So whaddaya say? Will you keep this to yourself?"

I promised not to breathe a word to Aunt Queenie, thus leaving myself free to tell Avanelle. For the umpteenth time, I wished she had a phone.

"Thanks, girlie. I'm indebted to you, like a turtle on a fence post."

What a weird thing to say. Maybe he *was* a tad bit off his rocker. Backing away from him, I said, "Wh-what?"

"It's an old saying. 'If you see a turtle sittin' on a fence post, you know he didn't get there by himself.' You never heard it?"

I shook my head.

"Well, think about it. Could a turtle climb a fence post?"

"No, but—but why would he want to?"

"That's just it. He wouldn't. Somebody put him up there against his will." Mr. Roebuck frowned. "My pa was a farmer, but he never had any use for tractors, and I reckon turtles and fence posts were the reasons why."

This was getting weirder by the minute. I didn't know whether to question the old man or shut the door in his face.

He must have seen my confusion, because he sighed impatiently and said, "Girlie, when I was a boy, most any farmer plowing with a tractor would pick up turtles and set 'em on fence posts, rather than smash 'em under the tires. At the end of the day, the farmer's kids would walk the fences and put the turtles back down on the ground."

I relaxed a bit. He was beginning to make sense.

"The neighbors right next to us—the Ingersols—had only the one boy," Mr. Roebuck went on, "and he was meaner than sin. He liked to leave one turtle stranded on a post. Every other day, my pa would send me to walk the fence row between our two properties just to check. I can't tell you how many times I'd find a turtle paddling thin air and waiting to die a slow death."

"And you saved him? Lifted him off the post?"

"You got it, girlie. All he needed was a little help from a friend," replied Mr. Roebuck, and he shuffled off down the hall.

I closed my door, and picked up a teddy bear blank. A

little help from a friend. That almost made me laugh. The turtle story didn't apply to Mr. Roebuck and me. We were definitely not friends.

Sure, he'd cut the blanks for me, but that didn't mean a thing. He'd done it to show Uncle Bert *he* wasn't afraid of machinery.

Cupping the blank in both hands, I savored its feathery weight and its faint scent of new wood. Dad had always cut my blanks before. I glanced at him in the family photo. His smiling face was tan and leathery—a farmer's face. Now there was a man who'd have moved a turtle to save it. He'd been careful with his livestock, good with the land. But in the end, the land hadn't been good to him, and he'd given up farming to become an antique dealer. I felt the crushing weight of sorrow, thinking of that ominous decision. His furniture trailer, loaded with antiques, had jackknifed behind the car, killing him and Mom instantly.

And now Heidi Grissom's grandfather was an antique *dabbler.*

A tiredness seeped through me, saturating every nerve and every pore. This day had been four days long.

I needed to unwind. Big time. I sat down, chose a knife from the Barbie case, and made the first rough cuts on that hunk of wood.

"Delrita, I'm home," said Aunt Queenie, knocking on the door.

"Come on in."

She swept in with a swirl of her purple skirt and the aroma of lilacs. "Hi. How was school today?"

"The police dog sniffed right past my locker, so I guess it was okay."

"I declare, Delrita," she said, crossing her arms across her lacy breast. "I never know what's going to come out of your mouth."

"Sorry. It was an awful day."

"And I suppose you don't want to talk about it."

"Not really."

"Have it your way. I came to ask if you'd clean out your closet sometime soon, because the community clothing bank needs kids' clothes."

"Sure. I've got lots of stuff I don't wear anymore."

Seeing the basswood in my hand, she said, "You're working on that bear for Joey Marcum."

"Just getting started."

Her blue eyes flickered toward the clowns on the dresser, then back to the bear. I knew she wanted to remind me again that Joey wasn't Punky, but she didn't. All she said was, "You can start as a Teen Buddy whenever you're ready. The director at the nursing home is flexible. She knows teenagers are busy, and she lets them pick their own schedules. You'll probably see the Marcums in the morning at Special Olympics, and you can arrange something then."

"Why can't I call Mrs. Marcum right now? See if Joey and I can get together tomorrow afternoon?"

"Suit yourself. But then I could use a hand with supper. I'm running late this evening, and you can dish up the peaches and cottage cheese."

Aunt Queenie left, and I stood grinning at the door. She

must have had a hard day, too, because she'd used the word *supper,* and that was such a backwoods expression.

Mrs. Marcum liked the idea of me being Joey's Teen Buddy. "Some kids are turned off by him," she said, "but you understand my Joey."

After setting it up for me to visit him the next afternoon, I thanked her and hung up.

Aunt Queenie brushed some crumbs off the countertop into her hand. "You certainly didn't have to twist her arm," she said.

"Who's that, Queen?" gargled Mr. Roebuck, coming up behind me.

"Lucille Marcum. Delrita's ready to start as Joey's Teen Buddy. She's already carving that bear for him."

He leveled that steely-eyed gaze at me. "Those blanks I cut were okay then?"

"They were fine, thanks. Sorry. I should have thanked you sooner."

"No problem, girlie." He lumbered past me, poured himself some coffee, and sat hunched over the mug at the table, like a stingy dog with a bone.

I could feel him watching me as I spooned cottage cheese into bowls and topped each mound with half a peach. I was setting the bowls in the refrigerator when he asked, "Whatcha gonna do with him?"

I let the door whoosh shut and stared at him blankly.

"With Joey?" he said. "How you gonna pass the time?"

"I don't know. See what he wants to do, I guess."

The old man frowned. "Don't figure on watching TV,

'cause he can stare at the tube by himself. And don't figure on doing crafts. I've asked him half a dozen times, but he never takes part."

No TV and no crafts. What did that leave? Counting the bubbles in the aquarium? Racing wheelchairs down the hall?

"Joey likes magic," he said.

"Magic? I don't know beans about magic."

"Joey'll take care of that. Just ask him to show you the 'magic' in his Magic Markers."

I remembered a TV program I'd seen about mentally disabled people who had remarkable talent in music and art. "You mean Joey's an artist?"

"You'll find out," said Mr. Roebuck.

His wily expression gave me the creeps. I didn't trust him, and I suddenly felt like the enemy again.

11

Special Olympics

I awoke to the sound of rain drumming on the roof. When I heard a door slam, I raised up enough to peek out the window and see Uncle Bert making a mad dash to his car parked on the street. He never carried an umbrella, and his toupee was getting soaked.

"Call the news," I murmured as I flopped back down. Punky had wanted me to call the news every time it rained, because he thought I could make the weatherman shut the water off.

Remembering it was Saturday, I pulled the blanket over my head. I had to psych myself up for Special Olympics.

Since Punky died, Special Olympics had become bittersweet. It was satisfying to help people challenged by disabilities. Yet it was painful, too, since many of the athletes had Down's syndrome and thus looked a lot like Punky. One man in particular—his friend Barney—even had the same personality. "My girl," Punky had called me a thousand times, and not a Saturday went by that Barney didn't ask me to be his wife.

In the cocoon of my covers, I pictured how Tree would "fight" with Barney over me. That boosted me out of bed and into the shower, though I still felt depressed.

Inch by inch, I did what I could to brighten my mood on this gloomy day. Instead of my white Special Olympics sweatshirt, I donned a T-shirt patterned all over with four-leaf clovers. I slipped on comfy Levi's and green socks with white Reeboks, tied green yarn around my ponytail, and applied a little blush to my cheeks. All the while, I centered my thoughts on Tree: mean machine on the football field; gentle giant at Special Olympics. At last, I felt able to cope. After a good-bye touch to the God's eye, I left the room.

As I walked down the hall, I could see Aunt Queenie sitting at the kitchen table. She was decked out in jeans, her Special Olympics sweatshirt, and tennis shoes, and her hair was tied low at the back of her neck. A white pencil was tucked behind her ear.

She looked younger without all her paint and polish, but she sounded the same. "I provided you with a spit can," she said to her father as I entered the kitchen, "so whatever possessed you to spit tobacco into my dieffenbachia?"

The old man swiveled in his chair and scowled at me.

"I didn't tell her," I said, sliding into my seat and reaching for the bran flakes.

"That dieffenbachia hasn't been the same since Punky pruned it down to a stub," Aunt Queenie said, "and now, even with extra love and plant food, it's probably going to die."

"A little tobacco juice won't hurt it," argued Mr. Roebuck. "It's done no harm to me."

"No harm? It turns your teeth yellow. It dribbles down your chin and stains your clothes. It's probably eating your insides as we speak."

My stomach did a flip-flop. I wasn't sure I could eat, but I went through the motions as the debate continued.

It was a draw. Aunt Queenie got her father to promise he'd stop spitting in the dieffenbachia, but judging from his smirk and shifty eyes, I knew his next target would be the philodendron.

It was pouring when Aunt Queenie honked at the Shacklefords' house. In the few seconds it took Tree and Avanelle to shoot out the door and into the backseat, they got drenched.

As we left the drive, I handed a box of tissues over the seat and sat sideways, watching them swab their faces. Their hair formed ringlets so tight, I was tempted to reach out and pull one, to see if it would "boing."

"Man, what a gully washer," said Avanelle.

"A little water won't hurt you," Tree said, patting her on the head. "It'll put curl in your hair."

She rolled her eyes at me. "Isn't he just too cute for words?"

"Y'all could try lovable," said Tree, slipping into his hillbilly drawl. "Or adorable. Irresistible. Fantabulous. Handsome. Remarkable. . . . Delrita, help me out here. I'm running out of adjectives."

I giggled. "You left out outrageous."

"Which reminds me," said Aunt Queenie, "I've heard glowing reports about the show you kids put on at the nursing home."

"I liked doing it," said Avanelle.

"No wonder," said Tree. "You got half the dough."

"Oh, quit belly-aching. The show is twice as good with me in it, so I deserve that fifty-fifty split."

"Which means you have to work for nothing this afternoon," Tree said.

Avanelle frowned at him. "Aren't we doing a surprise birthday party?"

"Yup, but it's for Coach's daughter, so it'll be a freebie."

"Trezane Shackleford, that's a dirty deal."

"No, it's a fifty-fifty split." Tree slapped his leg and broke up laughing. Aunt Queenie and I joined in, and finally, Avanelle did, too.

When we calmed down, I announced that I was officially Joey's Teen Buddy, and I told about his calls to nine-one-one. That set us off again.

"Hey, Velveeta," said Tree when we all stopped laughing, "maybe you could bring Joey to the party."

"I doubt if Mrs. Marcum would let me take him out of the nursing home. She barely knows me."

"She knows me," Aunt Queenie said. Fingering the pencil behind her ear, she addressed Tree in the rearview mirror. "You get permission from Coach Winslow. I'll handle Mrs. Marcum."

Aunt Queenie let us out under the canopy at the high school, then drove away to park the car. Since Avanelle had stopped at the rest room, Tree and I were alone in the hall-way, heading for the ruckus in the gym.

My thoughts were on Punky, who'd strutted like a champion after sinking a basketball through the net. I didn't realize I was frowning until Tree said, "I hope your face doesn't freeze that way."

I tried to smile. "I get uptight on Saturdays. That's when it really comes back to me—how much I miss everything. Punky, Mom and Dad, even the house."

Tree's freckled face turned red. "Sorry. I wasn't thinking."

"Forget it. I'll be okay after we get busy."

"Have you ever gone back? To the house, I mean."

"Just once, the night . . . of the accident. And I'll never, ever go again."

"I hear you," he said solemnly, sticking his hands in his pockets.

A minute later, we walked into the chaos of the gym—basketballs bouncing, wheelchairs rolling, people talking and laughing and milling in a sea of white sweatshirts.

All but Joey. He was sitting with his mother on the front row of the bleachers, halfway across the gym. Under the lights, his curls were golden, his broad face ghostly white. He would have looked like one of the crowd in his white sweatshirt and jogging pants, if not for the belt with the Elvis buckle, the bright red boots on his feet, and the teddy bear in his lap.

"My wife!" cried a familiar voice, and I scanned the crowd for Barney, the man who reminded me so much of Punky.

Short legs churning like pistons, he scurried up to us in

his bib overalls and cowboy hat. "My wife," he wheezed with a blinding smile. "Give me five."

I slapped his palm as Tree said, "Listen, Barn, she can't marry you. She's my girl."

"My wife, buster," argued Barney, bellying up to him.

Tree threw an arm across my shoulders. "Nope. My girl."

Barney tried to pull me away, but Tree held on tight.

It was impossible to feel sad while being fought over in a tug-of-war. I was giggling by the time Coach blew his whistle.

"Saved by the bell, Barn," said Tree.

"Fwiends," Barney said and gave him five.

Tree headed for the opposite end of the gym to referee relay races, but I could still feel the weight and the warmth of his arm across my shoulders.

Soon Aunt Queenie was hugging everyone who made the effort in the basketball toss, while Avanelle and I fetched stray balls.

When the last whistle blew, Tree trotted up to me, his face sweaty, his hair clumped in damp ringlets. "Hey, Velveeta," he panted, "Coach gave the go-ahead for you and Joey to attend the party. Now all we need is permission from Joey's mom."

How I wanted to touch those ringlets, but I moved away, saying, "I'll get Aunt Queenie."

I found her in the locker room, tending to Susie Grotzinger, who'd stumbled against a wall in the gym. Aunt Queenie's shirt was spattered with red, and her hair was coming loose from its ribbon.

"You're fine now, hon," she said as she wiped Susie's face with a clean wet towel. "The bleeding's stopped."

"I'm not gonna die?" snuffled Susie.

"Not from a bloody nose."

"Just wait till I tell Connie," said an indignant Susie. Then she hugged Aunt Queenie, kissed her on the cheek, and bounded past me out the door.

I told Aunt Queenie about Coach's okay, and we hurried to catch the Marcums. They were already outside under the canopy, and Joey was guiding his mother's wheelchair onto the lift of the nursing home van.

He babbled with concern when he saw the blood on Aunt Queenie's shirt. I figured if he had a phone, he'd be dialing nine-one-one.

Aunt Queenie assured him she was fine, but he kept his good eye riveted on her while she talked to his mother.

"I'm sorry, no," said Mrs. Marcum as she adjusted the bandanna on Peanut's neck so it would hold his head up. "I know I'm overprotective, but Joey's all I have."

Aunt Queenie pestered her until the "no" became a "yes."

"Ya, ya, ya!" Joey jabbered, dripping a little drool in his excitement. He hurled himself at Aunt Queenie and hugged her so hard, they both almost fell down.

"Well, I declare," she cried, quickstepping to catch her balance.

A peevish thought crossed my mind: That's the way it is on Saturdays. Everybody but me hugs the queen.

Rain poured and thunder boomed as Aunt Queenie drove into the garage. When we entered the house and heard Orvis Roebuck's voice in the family room, I knew he was recording his war stories and wasn't aware we'd come in.

Raising her eyebrows at me, Aunt Queenie said, "That's odd. He hates using the phone." I was right behind her when she marched into the family room. "Is that for me, Pop?"

The old man jerked in his chair as though he'd been shot. "Queen," he roared, "don't sneak up on me like that." Slick as a whistle, he slid a newspaper off the table and onto his lap.

"Who was that on the phone?"

"Nobody. I was—uh—just—reading the paper."

"Out loud?"

"I was lonesome. Needed to hear a friendly voice."

"Well, I declare. Talking to yourself."

"A man has to talk to somebody. You're too danged busy. Always running off somewhere."

"I have commitments, Pop, including a meeting with the blood drive volunteers this afternoon. But Delrita and I will keep you company at lunch, just as soon as I freshen up."

"You look just fine to me. Real natural, instead of like a department store dummy."

"Well, I declare, Pop. I just declare," said Aunt Queenie as she sashayed out of the room.

I couldn't help but smile at the old man.

He winked at me, lifted the paper, and tapped the tape recorder. "Thanks, girlie. I owe you one."

Hard to figure. Two days ago, I couldn't stand being close to him, and now here I was, keeping a secret for him.

I washed up, donned a clean green shirt, and redid my ponytail before going into the kitchen. I was arranging low-fat cheese and turkey ham on a plate when Aunt Queenie came in. Her hair was back in its topknot, her face was painted on, and she'd changed into a flowered dress with a red belt and red shoes.

She looked like a mannequin. I smiled to myself, remembering Mr. Roebuck's description. Imagine calling your own daughter a department store dummy.

12

Joey's Magic

At Rest Haven, I waited under the canopy while Aunt Queenie parked the car. Soon she came puddle-jumping through the rain under her flowered umbrella. Inside, as she set the umbrella next to a couple more that were dripping on a rug, the aquarium belched like a gassy old man.

The smell of the place was slightly different, but not improved. Ancient bodies, medicine, meatloaf. I spied two Teen Buddies in action—a boy playing dominoes with a bald-headed man, and a girl painting the fingernails of a tiny, shriveled woman. Down the hall, someone was yelling over and over, "My ironing board. Where'd you hide my ironing board?"

I wanted to hurry in and hurry out, but that wasn't possible with Aunt Queenie, who talked to everyone we met: "Mr. Beesley, how's that arthritis? . . . Miss Whitfield, you have a new perm. . . . Well, I declare, Calvin. No wonder you're stuck. How'd you get your lap robe tangled up in that wheel?"

We made our way past rooms so monotonous, I had the sensation of moving without going anywhere. Tan bedspreads, tan drapes, tan chairs.

What a terrible place to live, I thought, anxious to find Joey and take him out of here.

When we turned a corner, I collided with someone and caught a book in the stomach. "Oooof," I grunted, clutching my middle as the book hit the floor. Of all things, it was a treasury of nursery rhymes.

"I'm sorry," said a girl, bending down to pick it up.

Hot pink jogging suit, musk cologne, a cloud of blond hair. Heidi Grissom. When she looked up, my first thought was that she failed the cherub test today, because her round cheeks were pale as dough. My next thought was that she must be a Teen Buddy to someone experiencing a second childhood. Why else would she be hauling around Little Miss Muffet and Humpty Dumpty?

"Delrita," she said, "did I hurt you? Guess I should watch where I'm going."

"I'll live."

She flashed a smile at Aunt Queenie. "You must be Delrita's aunt. I'm Heidi Grissom."

"Grissom? I don't recognize the name."

"I just moved here with my grandparents—the Naramores."

"Oh, my," said Aunt Queenie, raising her eyebrows as that name registered in her brain. For once, she seemed at a loss for words. What do you say to the girl who stepped into the life your niece left behind?

She didn't have to say anything, because Heidi jumped right in and said to me, "I'm glad I ran into you today."

Very funny, considering she'd deflated me with those nursery rhymes.

"I was going to call you," she said.

"You were?" I peeped. I didn't get many calls, but Heidi Grissom was the last person I'd want to hear on the other end of the line. I could just imagine how she'd sit on the countertop in the kitchen, swinging her legs and fiddling with the telephone cord.

Heidi nodded. "About the history assignment."

"What assignment is that, Delrita?" asked Aunt Queenie.

I couldn't think my way out of this, so I had to tell her about the interviews.

She smiled at Heidi and said, "My father's a combat veteran."

"I know. Avanelle told me about him yesterday after school."

I saw what was coming, and I wanted to run, but I just stood there feeling my face grow hot.

"Anyway, Delrita," said Heidi, "I needed to check with you about Mr. Roebuck. Avanelle said you weren't going to interview him, and if that's the case, I want him for myself."

"There must be some mistake," said Aunt Queenie with a bewildered glance at me. "Of course Delrita will interview my father. He's not only a combat veteran, but a re-tired master sergeant with a distinguished service record."

I felt my stomach sink to my knees. It was either inter-view Orvis Roebuck or insult Aunt Queenie. I heaved a sigh. "I—uh—I do plan to interview him. I just hadn't got-ten around to asking him yet."

Heidi sighed, too. "Then I'll have to find somebody else."

"You might try the VFW," suggested Aunt Queenie.

"I will. I just wanted to talk to Delrita first."

It was on the tip of my tongue to say, "Well, you've talked to me, so get lost." But I couldn't be rude with Aunt Queenie watching. I focused on Heidi's book and asked, "Do you read to somebody?"

"Yeah. To a woman down there," she said, indicating the hall behind her. "Well, I should be going. My ride's probably here."

"Nice meeting you," said Aunt Queenie.

"You, too. 'Bye, Delrita. See you at school."

When Heidi disappeared around the corner, I expected Aunt Queenie to ask a dozen questions. Instead, she checked her watch and said, "We'd better get Joey. Tree and Avanelle might give up on us, and I don't want them walking in the rain."

She led the way past more rooms done in drab decor. At the last door on the left, she stopped to let me enter first.

I stared, open-mouthed and goggle-eyed. The room was an oasis. Red bedspreads, TV set, Elvis posters, the smell of peppermint. Peanut perched on his own little bamboo chair beneath a helium balloon. Mrs. Marcum, in a cone of lamplight, reading in her wheelchair by the window.

Perched cross-legged in the center of a bed was Joey, wearing earphones and applying Magic Marker to a page in a sketch pad.

"We're here," said Aunt Queenie, knocking on the door, and I managed to shut my mouth and follow her when Mrs. Marcum said, "Come in."

She propelled herself toward us by groping at the spread on the empty bed. "Joey's so excited. He whisked me out of the dining hall before I finished lunch." Tapping him on the arm, she asked, "Are you ready, son?"

He shook his head, keeping his eyes on the paper.

"Never disturb an artist at work," said Mrs. Marcum, smiling at me.

I eased over to the bed. The "magic" in the marker was turning the page from white to green. No pictures, no symbols. Just green.

"You're being very meticulous, Joey," said Aunt Queenie.

No response. He kept working the marker until the last bit of white had disappeared. Then he exchanged the green marker for a black one and scrawled big, uneven block letters at the bottom of the page: MRJOEYMARCUM.

Mr. Joey Marcum. It was disturbing somehow, that "mister" in front of his name. I blinked hard to stop the stinging in my eyes.

Off came the earphones, and the muffled voice of Elvis

Presley floated through the air. Joey tore the page carefully on the perforated line and placed it in my hands.

"For me?"

"Ya," he said, climbing off the bed.

"Thanks. Green's my favorite color."

"We guessed right then," said Mrs. Marcum. "Easy enough. We've seen you a couple of times wearing green."

When Joey handed Aunt Queenie a bag of peppermints tied with red yarn, his mother said, "He wanted to give the little girl a present."

Boy, oh, boy. Joey was light-years ahead of me. I hadn't even thought about a present.

He tucked the tail of his blue-striped cowboy shirt into his jeans and centered the Elvis buckle. He was putting on a red cowboy boot when he noticed Aunt Queenie's red shoes. "Ya, ya, ya," he said, and pointed at her feet.

To my utter amazement, she danced a circle around him, kicking and tapping in her high heels. This from a woman without a frivolous bone in her body.

Joey giggled and gave her five. Then he lifted Peanut from the bamboo chair, kissed his mother good-bye, and took my hand.

"Delrita?" said Mrs. Marcum as we were leaving.

I stopped and looked back at her. "Yes, ma'am?"

"Take good care of my boy."

At that moment, it struck me that I could be making a big mistake. What if the kids at the birthday party were cruel to Joey or afraid of him? What if he suffered a spell with his heart?

I wished I'd considered those possibilities before committing myself, but it was too late to back out now.

In the car, Joey rode up front with Aunt Queenie. I sat in the back and stared at the picture he'd given me.

MRJOEYMARCUM. That "mister" was really bothering me. Joey was a little boy, twenty-three years old, and it was up to me to take care of him for a couple of hours.

How would I react if someone mistreated him at the party? I'd probably freeze up, just like I had when I ran into Heidi. Freezing up was a habit with me. When I needed most to speak out, I'd get all flustered and tongue-tied. I'd allowed myself to be railroaded by Heidi, and now I was stuck with interviewing Mr. Roebuck.

At Avanelle's house, sequins flashed as she poked her head out the door and signaled *just a minute.* The minute stretched into two or three, so I borrowed Aunt Queenie's umbrella and splashed over to McDonald's to buy some gift coupons for Andrea, the coach's daughter.

When Aunt Queenie drove around to pick me up, Outrageous was in the back seat—and so was Joey. Nose mashed against the watery window, he was grinning at me. His happiness was contagious, and I felt my spirits lift as I scooted into the front seat beside Avanelle.

A crazy potpourri of smells hit me—wet heads, peppermint, cologne, hair spray, starch, and greasepaint.

"Weeta!" said Joey, and he nudged my shoulder with Peanut before waggling him at Tree.

Outrageous winked at me and grinned, revealing his

blacked-out front teeth. It occurred to me then that Joey didn't know it was Tree under all that makeup. To me, the real magic of Joey was his childlike innocence.

Coach Winslow was waiting for us in his garage, and he dashed out to help unload the props. "You're just what the doctor ordered," he said as Aunt Queenie drove away and Tree slipped off his shoes. "So far, this party's a flop. No games, no excitement. Everybody's watching a video in the basement."

He led us through the garage and down some steps, saying, "It's a terrible thing to see—a bunch of eight-year-old couch potatoes. I thought about making them run laps and do pushups, but the wife said no."

"Have you got any grapefruit?" asked Tree.

"Grapefruit?" Coach stopped so fast that Tree bumped into him, and Joey bumped into Tree. It's a wonder they didn't land in a heap at the bottom of the steps.

"For a relay race," said Tree. "Guaranteed to get spuds off the couch."

"Oh." Coach sounded doubtful, but when we reached the bottom of the stairs, he went back up for the grapefruit.

We were in a recreation room decorated for a party that had no fizz. Boys and girls in pointy hats sat as if hypnotized, staring at the tube. Mrs. Winslow thanked us for the gift coupons and the bag of peppermints, but none of the kids even glanced our way.

She clapped her hands. "Heads up, everyone. Look who's here."

All eyes turned toward us. Faces registered surprise, then delight, when the kids saw Outrageous.

"Hey, Mom, look! A clown!" exclaimed Andrea, the birthday girl.

Tree bowed and swept off his floppy hat. "Outrageous is the name, and fun is the game."

All the kids swarmed around him like bees around a rosebush.

Quick as a flash, the mood changed when Joey squeezed into their huddle. Two little girls backed away from him, their eyes wide with fear. A boy with thick glasses asked rudely, "What's he doing here?"

The question hung in the air. Mrs. Winslow and Avanelle were statues with frozen smiles. Joey fidgeted, one shoulder drooping, but he was smiling, too—a puzzled smile that seemed to say, What's the matter? I just want to play.

Say something, I told myself, but I was tongue-tied with anger. Feeling the old, familiar helplessness, I shot a glance at Tree. He was still holding his hat, and he fiddled with its brim as he eyed the kids' leery faces.

"It's okay, kids," he said at last, ramming the hat onto his head. "Joey's a friend of mine."

"He's too old for a teddy bear," piped one little girl.

"What's wrong with his eyes?" said the boy with the glasses. "He must be dumb. Just look at that slobber on his chin."

"Joey's special," retorted Andrea, "and *you're* the one who's dumb."

Andrea's words brought her mother back to life. "Children," she said, "where are your manners? We invited the clown and his friends here to join in the fun."

"That's right," said Tree. Dragging his bare foot across

the carpet, he drew an imaginary line. "Anybody who wants to have a good time, step over this line."

Avanelle was first, followed by Andrea, Joey, and four of the kids. The others stood still, staring at Joey.

"That's seven," said Tree. "I need one more to make it even."

As I opened my mouth to volunteer, Coach said, "I'll play," and tossed a couple of grapefruit to Tree.

"Okay, everyone," Tree said, "watch while Outrageous demonstrates how this relay race works." Holding a grapefruit with his knees, he hobbled to the far end of the room, touched the wall, and hobbled back. "Pass the grapefruit to the next person in the line, but without using your hands. If you drop it, you have to start over."

A few more kids moved up to play, crossing the line but staying as far away from Joey as possible. To even out the number, I joined Joey's team.

The kids got so involved in the race, they forgot all about Joey, until he came up last to carry the grapefruit. Clutching Peanut under one arm and the grapefruit between his mismatched knees, he moved slowly, awkwardly, ignoring all of us who were yelling at him to hurry.

Meanwhile, Avanelle, hustling for the other team, lost her grapefruit and had to start over. It was all the advantage Joey needed. He kept plugging along, and he won the race. When our team cheered and slapped him on the back, his smile lit up the room.

A loud pop sounded, and heads jerked around. There stood Tree, feigning surprise that he'd popped a balloon. "We've still got some party poopers," he said, "so we're gonna liven up the next race by using balloons instead of grapefruit. If you break your balloon, start over."

This time, every child stepped over the imaginary line.

Our team lost that race, but you'd never have known it, because Joey gave everybody five.

"Now that you're in the party mood," said Tree, "Outrageous can do what he came for. Pull up a seat on the floor and watch. You're about to see a show that will knock your socks off."

The kids were all giggling as they parked themselves on the carpet. The boy with the glasses said, "Over here, Joey. You can sit by me."

13

A Soul
in Limbo

When Coach and Mrs. Winslow left with a van full of kids to take home, my group waited in the garage for Aunt Queenie. Joey sat on a toolbox, watching the rain, while the rest of us stood at the door.

"You'll never guess who I ran into at the nursing home," I said.

"Who?" asked Avanelle.

"Heidi Grissom." I kept an eye on Tree to see if he'd perk up at the name.

His expression didn't change under the makeup.

When I told how Heidi had backed me into a corner, Avanelle said, "I should have kept my big trap shut. She walked part of the way with me to Miss Myrtle's house yesterday, and I talked too much. I figured if I didn't let her get a word in edgewise, I wouldn't have to listen to her bragging."

Tree pulled his red bandanna from the bib of his over-alls and waved it at his sister like a flag in front of a bull.

She ignored him.

"How come you're always snorting and stomping about Heidi?" he asked. "What'd she ever do to you?"

When Avanelle didn't answer, he said, "It's the clothes, isn't it? You don't like her because of her nice clothes."

"You are so dense," she said, turning her back on him.

"I was right. It's the clothes."

Avanelle crossed her arms and glared at him over her shoulder.

"Truce," he said as a white car with its lights on nosed into the drive.

It was Uncle Bert in his Lincoln. His face was distorted by the watery windshield, and he looked grouchy.

After tossing the prop boxes into the trunk, we climbed into the car. I was careful to sit in the back this time, between Tree and Joey.

Something was wrong. I knew it when Uncle Bert began backing up while we were still sorting safety belts.

"Queenie's on her way to Jefferson City," he said.

I focused on a vein throbbing in his neck. "Jeff City? I thought she had a meeting."

"She's headed for the hospital. Evidently, Orvis went out in a downpour to get the mail and fell flat on the driveway. We don't know how long he was there before Ruth Cable saw him and called the ambulance."

"Oh." I cringed at the picture of Mr. Roebuck lying helpless in the cold rain.

"Was he hurt bad?" asked Tree.

"It's for sure he broke his leg, and I expect there's the danger of pneumonia. I'll know more when I get to the hospital."

Avanelle looked back at me, and I read the message on her face: A broken leg and possible pneumonia. You won't be interviewing him.

"I called the preacher, first thing," Uncle Bert said. "Queenie wanted Orvis on the prayer list."

Joey was swiping at the rainwater on one of his boots with his stubby fingers. The droplets moved around, but they didn't go away.

"Here, pardner. Try this," Tree said, offering his bandanna.

"Ya!" Joey snatched it up and rubbed it across his boot.

We rode in silence then, except for the whoosh of the windshield wipers and the smack of the tires rolling through water.

Disturbing pictures scrolled across the screen of my mind. Orvis Roebuck on a stretcher in an ambulance. Punky in the hospital, in intensive care. Aunt Queenie driving like a wild woman to get us there. Me watching the clock on the waiting room wall, feeling helpless, hopeless.

The rain intensified, and Uncle Bert turned the wipers up full blast. As he hunched forward, straining to see the road, the back of his toupee jutted out from his scalp. "A few minutes wouldn't have made that much difference," he muttered. "I would have driven her as soon as I closed up the office, but she couldn't wait."

The big car hit a gully of water and swerved slightly. I

had a vision of Aunt Queenie's car hydroplaning . . . veering out of control on the rain-slick highway. My stomach tightened.

I must have made a sound, because Tree reached over and took my hand. I stared at our fingers, intertwined. Mine were long and pale and skinny. His were short and freckled and strong. Mine were cold, while his were warm. Opposites. Opposites attract, I told myself, trying to force my thoughts away from car accidents and . . . death.

We had pulled into the Shacklefords' drive. Joey elbowed me, held up the bandanna, and pointed to the one on Peanut's neck.

I stared at him, uncomprehending.

Tree squeezed my hand, then let it go. "He's showing you they're just alike." To Joey, he said, "I've got another one in the house. That one's yours to keep."

"Ya."

As Tree climbed from the car, Joey thrust the bandanna into my lap and pointed again at Peanut.

I tied the bandanna around Joey's neck.

"Ya," he said, and beamed at me like a carefree little boy.

I smiled back at him. The man of few words had lightened my load with nothing but a grin.

At the nursing home, Uncle Bert kept the engine running.

"I'll hurry," I promised as Joey and I got out of the car.

But Mr. Joey Marcum couldn't be hurried. He shuffled along in his side-to-side gait, stopping to admire his reflection in the glass of the aquarium. As we journeyed through the building, he showed off his bandanna to everyone we met.

When we turned the corner into his home stretch, he stopped again to preen before a mirror.

A hissing sound made me curious and drew me down the hall. What I found was a woman hooked up to machines in a private room, her body so wasted, it barely made a rumple under the covers. Her thick, chestnut-colored braid suggested youth, but her appearance was that of a crone. She was lying on her back, eyes closed, her nose as thin and sharp as a bird's beak. Tubes ran to her nose and her matchstick arms, and I gathered they were keeping her alive.

I shivered. Would this woman ever get well, or would she remain like this until she died—a soul in limbo? How helpless her family must feel. No watching the clock for them. They'd be marking the calendar by months. Maybe years. . . .

"M-m-my mama," said Joey with a tug on my arm. Now that we were close to his mother, he wanted *me* to hurry.

I thought about the comatose woman as we zipped past more doorways. How'd she end up in that condition? A car accident? Disease? A fall?

Joey and I burst into his room, startling Mrs. Marcum, who was dozing in her wheelchair. "M-m-my m-mama!" he exclaimed, and hugged her as if he'd been gone for a week.

I realized then that Joey was happy living in the nursing home—would be happy anywhere, as long as he had his mama.

"Did you have a good time, son?"

"Ya."

Mrs. Marcum looked to me for the details, so I gave her a couple of highlights. I even told her the kids had been afraid of Joey, but that he'd won them over.

While heading back up the hall, I glanced again at the comatose woman. The nameplate on her door read "Madeline Zang." Was she somebody's mama?

It was strange, but I felt wiser on my way out than I had on my way in. The smells of food and medicine and old folks didn't seem as repulsive as they had a while ago. I decided I could be happy anywhere—even in this nursing home—if only I had my mama.

14

A Giant
Hershey's Kiss

Uncle Bert drove into Aunt Queenie's spot in the garage to let me out. As I opened the car door, the faint aroma of wood smoke told me that someone nearby was using a fireplace. How I loved that homey smell, but I knew it wasn't coming from our house. That stack of boxes on the woodpile had been there since Christmas.

"Sure you don't want to go with me?" asked Uncle Bert.

"I'm sure. Hospitals give me the creeps."

"Well, okay, but you'll be by yourself till late. Be sure and keep all the doors locked, and call the Cables if you have a problem."

"Don't worry about me. Go on and see about Mr. Roebuck. Be extra careful, since the roads are wet."

"I'll be careful." Uncle Bert chucked me under the chin. "I've got to come back and take care of my girl."

My girl—Punky's term for me.

My girl. My girl. The words kept time with the rain as I headed for the house.

The door between the garage and the kitchen was un-locked—a sign that Aunt Queenie had left in a hurry to see about her dad. Remembering the newscast about the break-ins, I stepped inside warily and listened. No sound except for the humming of the fridge and the pounding of the rain.

Lights were on in the kitchen and family room. Aunt Queenie's umbrella lay in a little puddle by the phone, and on the table was the "magic" picture I'd left in her car. After hanging the umbrella in the garage, I locked the door and turned off the kitchen light. Then I took the Magic Marker masterpiece to my room, thumbtacked it above my desk, and wandered back out to the hall.

The light in the family room beckoned, so I decided to work on Joey's bear in there and watch TV. A company living room, a cold fireplace—yet Aunt Queenie let me carve anywhere I wanted to as long as I used a tarp to catch my wood shavings. Another example of a paradox.

I fetched the tarp and my Barbie case and towel, and arranged them on the floor. As I reached for the TV's re-mote control, I saw Mr. Roebuck's tape recorder on his chair. So he'd been telling war stories before going out to fetch the mail. Again, I pictured him lying helpless in the rain, and his voice echoed in my mind: "You know how Queen is. Once she gets hold of something, she won't let it go."

It was up to me to hide the evidence. I could think of only one place in the whole house that would be safe from

Aunt Queenie on a cleaning binge—Mr. Roebuck's duffel bag. Did I dare enter the old man's room? If I did, he would accuse me of snooping. If I didn't, Aunt Queenie would want to know every little detail of what he was recording and why, and then she'd pester him to attend that reunion and write that book.

With a sigh, I picked up the tape recorder and carried it down the hall to the room I hadn't set foot in since Mr. Roebuck moved in.

It had once been a beautiful blue and white guest room, but now the bedspread and draperies were a practical black-and-tan plaid. Magazines and newspapers lay haphazardly on the nightstand, along with a tobacco pouch and a pocketknife. A few grains of tobacco and a scrap of cellophane lay on the vanilla carpet. Other than that, the room was military neat. Framed certificates and army photos hung on the walls, and an UNCLE SAM WANTS YOU poster hung on the closet door. The spread looked tight enough to bounce a quarter off the bed.

The duffel bag wasn't in sight, and I recalled Mr. Roebuck saying he'd put it away so Aunt Queenie wouldn't have to look at it. Now what? I didn't want to rummage around in the old man's room, any more than I wanted him rummaging around in mine. My gaze swept the area. No duffel bag. But an object on the dresser caught my eye. I eased over and picked it up. It was the swan I'd tossed into the wastebasket. The wing had been glued back on.

Since the repair job didn't show, I ran my finger over the crack to make sure it was there. It was, of course, and I set the carving back on the dresser.

Why would an old army sergeant want that swan? Why would he mend the broken wing? I shook my head and scanned the room again. The duffel bag had to be in the closet.

The stern-faced Uncle Sam pointed an accusing finger at me as I approached the closet and opened the door.

Mr. Roebuck's shirts and trousers hung in a neat row on the rod, but the aroma of cedar couldn't mask the odor of dust and old metal coming from the lumpy canvas bag on the floor. The bag lay slumped against the wall like a wounded soldier, and when I opened it, the army helmet inside added to the illusion of a fallen man.

As I pushed at the helmet to make room for the recorder, I realized it was not one helmet, but two, stacked together. Two helmets? Unless a man had two heads, he didn't need two helmets. With a twinge of guilt—because I really was snooping now—I pulled them out for a closer look. The bottom helmet had a dent on one side. A dent caused by a bullet?

A prickle traveled up my spine. Had the fellow who'd worn that helmet been killed in combat? Who was he? And why would Orvis Roebuck keep such a grim reminder of war?

I put the helmets back, added the recorder, and closed the bag, feeling somehow as if I were sealing up the ghost of a dead soldier. After shutting the closet door, I glanced again at the swan on the dresser. Then, thoroughly mystified, I hurried out of the room.

All at once, the house seemed cavernous, and I almost wished I'd ridden to the hospital with Uncle Bert, just so I wouldn't be alone. The endless hammering of rain on the roof was an irritating sound. I thought of Punky, asking me to "call the news," and I thought of Mom laughing at Dad, because the drumming of rain always put him to sleep in his chair.

Sadness seeped through me like a chill. I turned on the lights and closed all the drapes in the kitchen, dining room, and family room, just so I wouldn't have to look at the rain drizzling down the windowpanes. That didn't accomplish much, except make me feel isolated from the world. A fire in the fireplace would have helped, but I wasn't sure I could start one from scratch, and I might end up smoking myself out of the house. Not to mention that I'd have to polish the furniture later because the ashes would create dust.

In the family room, I channel-surfed, hoping to find a good movie. The shows all looked like no-brainers, so I switched the TV off and the radio on—just in time to hear a newscast that added to my unrest: "At least two people are involved in the rash of burglaries in Tangle Nook. Late last night, a neighbor saw the thief running from a victim's house into an alley, where an accomplice was waiting in a pickup. Police are looking for a burly man of undetermined age, as well as an old, dark-colored Ford pickup with a camper shell and a knock in the engine. They caution all residents to lock their doors. . . ."

I double-checked all the doors and windows, then settled down with Joey's bear. As I worked, unwelcome images played themselves in my mind. Mr. Roebuck lying injured on the driveway. A soldier lying dead in a foxhole.

A woman hiding in a closet. Heidi Grissom's clothes hanging in *my* closet.

Too bad I can't switch channels in my brain, I thought, and kept shaving away at Joey's bear.

I had carved the body and was forming the feet with a V-tool when the ring of the doorbell scared me. I hadn't heard a car, and it was still raining, so who could it be? Mrs. Cable from across the street? A burglar?

Don't be a dodo, I told myself on the way to the living room. No burglar would be dumb enough to choose a house with lights on and politely ring the bell.

Cautiously, I peered through the peephole. Since darkness was gathering, I could see only a great, hulking shadow on the porch. When I turned on the light, I saw it was Tree, his bulky body covered by a brown garbage bag and his head protected by his white Outrageous hat. He looked so silly, and I was so relieved, I laughed out loud as I flung open the door.

"That's gratitude for you," he said to the porch roof. "Come to rescue a fair maiden and she laughs in your face."

"I'm sorry," I giggled. "Come on in."

"Better not. I'll drip all over the place."

"It's only water. Come on."

Tree entered the house and stood towering over me on the welcome mat. I couldn't think what to say to him, so I just stood there grinning.

"Are you fixing to laugh at me again?" he asked.

"Probably. You look like a giant Hershey's Kiss." As soon as the words were out, my face grew hot enough to melt chocolate.

Tree's emerald eyes were twinkling, and his freckled cheeks were rounded with a smile. "A Hershey's Kiss, huh?" he said, and kissed me on the forehead.

I nearly fainted from shock and pleasure. Surely his lips had seared a hole in my face. I wanted to touch the spot, but I couldn't move—not even to blink.

Tree misinterpreted my reaction, and he shifted uneasily. "Hey, Velveeta, I'm sorry. I shouldn't have done that."

"I—you—it's all right. I just wasn't expecting it, that's all."

"I really am sorry. It's just that—well, you reminded me of Birdie, standing there all big-eyed and innocent. You just looked kissable."

Now I was totally confused. I liked being "kissable," but I wasn't sure it was flattering to be compared to a four-year-old. "Uh—what's this about rescuing me?"

"Mom sent me to get you. She says the weather's too dreary for you to be by yourself, and she's been hearing about those break-ins. If you've got a sleeping bag, bring it. Mom and Dad moved out to the porch today, but we're still short on beds. Too many house apes at the Shackleford Zoo."

I'd never stayed the night at the Shacklefords' house, but I knew it would be an adventure. "Give me five minutes to get ready. No, make that three. And have a seat while you wait."

Tree hesitated, glancing at the blue and cream sectional sofa lining two walls and the tables gleaming with wax.

"Go ahead and sit," I said. "This living room's for company, and you're it."

"I'd better just stand here on the mat. Water on the floor is one thing, but wet upholstery is another."

"Okay, but I'll hurry." I streaked into the family room, bundled all my carving supplies into the tarp, stashed it behind the couch, and turned off the lights. In my room, I dug out my sleeping bag, then loaded my backpack with a jogging suit to sleep in, toiletries, Bible, and the clothes I'd need for church in the morning.

"Almost ready," I said as I dumped my things in the living room before racing into the kitchen. I scribbled a note on the bulletin board, and I left a coded message on the answering machine to tell Aunt Queenie where I was: "Hi! This is Delrita Jensen. I can't come to the phone right now, because I'm watching the *Birdies* in the *Trees.*"

"I like that," called Tree. "One point for the good guys, and zip for the burglars."

I grinned in his direction. After fetching my raincoat and Aunt Queenie's umbrella from the garage, I tore into the living room and lurched to a stop before him.

When he bent toward me, I didn't dare breathe. He was going to kiss me again! No, he reached for the sleeping bag and pulled it up under the garbage bag. "I know," he said. "Now I look like a lumpy Hershey's Kiss."

My face was flaming as I donned my coat and picked up the backpack.

"You know," Tree said, "this is really far out."

"What is?"

"Your place is loaded with furniture, but you're going to my house, where some of us will have to stand up at supper, and you'll have to sleep on the floor."

I swept an arm around the living room. "Do you feel at home here?"

"Not really," he said.

"Neither do I."

We were silent then, while Tree measured me with his eyes.

"You've heard the saying, 'It takes a heap of living to make a house a home'?" I said. "I don't think furniture makes any difference."

He scratched his head and gave that some thought. "I hear you, but Avanelle might not. When I left, she was polishing the paint off Miss Mabel's dresser."

"She got it?"

"This afternoon. It looks real nice, but don't tell her I said so. I made fun of the dinky little stool that came with it."

"You're terrible."

"I know. Birdie called me an old meanie. Said I should be glad we had an extra chair."

Laughing, we walked onto the porch. After switching the backpack to my other arm, I opened the umbrella and held it over both our heads as we ventured out into the rain.

By the time we'd run out of sidewalk, Tree had matched his pace with mine, and we moved along the roadway in perfect step.

I savored the clean, damp smell of him, combined with the aromas of wood smoke and suppers being cooked. I thought how beautiful the streetlights were, shimmering on wet pavement.

"Brrrr, it's getting colder," Tree said. "Mom's chili's gonna hit the spot."

"My dad was the chili maker at our house. He called it 'blue flame,' because it would set you on fire."

Tree chuckled. "Your dad set fire to the chili. Mine set fire to the chairs."

"The chairs?"

"When we lived in St. Louis, Dad was a laborer for the railroad. Worked outside all year long in scorching sun and freezing cold. Some nights he'd come home chilled to the bone. He'd sit astraddle a chair on the floor furnace until he thawed out or the legs caught fire, whichever came first. Didn't you ever notice that our chairs' legs are charred at the bottom?"

"No."

"Well, they are. Every once in a while, a leg breaks off, and another chair bites the dust."

Our laughter echoed through the night, and the air smelled like a wooden chair going up in smoke.

15

Secrets

The lights were on, the curtains open, so Tree and I had a straight shot into his living room. We saw Mr. Shackleford wrestling with Randolph and Eddie, Birdie tottering past them with the baby on her hip, and Gordy playing trampoline on the couch.

Tree stopped on the porch to peel off his garbage bag, then opened the door. "Ta-dah," he announced. "Delrita-Velveeta's here."

Birdie turned so quickly that the baby keeled backward. Ellie saved herself from falling by snatching a handful of Birdie's hair.

"Ouch!" howled Birdie. "She's pulling *hard!*"

I dropped the backpack and rescued her by grabbing the baby and prying her fat little fingers loose.

"I've got a secret," said Birdie as she rubbed her sore spot.

"Birdie!" yelled Mrs. Shackleford from the kitchen.

"But I'm not s'posed to tell it yet," added Birdie, looking pleased with herself.

From the girls' bedroom, Avanelle called, "Come in and see my boudoir."

The room was cramped with furniture—a crib, a double bed that sagged in the middle, the cardboard box table, an old chest of drawers, and the "new" vanity dresser with its large round mirror and wire-legged stool.

"This is beautiful," I said, touching the dresser's smooth, white- and gold-painted wood.

"French provincial," said Avanelle. "That's what makes this a boudoir."

Sticking his head in the doorway, Tree plunked my backpack onto the floor. "That thing weighs a ton," he said. "Better not set it on that dinky little stool."

"You . . . are . . . such . . . a . . . pain," said Avanelle, punching out each word.

Tree winked at me and disappeared.

Ellie was wriggling and poking her fingers into my mouth, so I shifted her in my arms.

"The little rascal's heavy," said Avanelle. "Let's put her in her high chair. It's time for me to set the table."

We went to the kitchen, and I zeroed in on the chairs. The bottom three or four inches of each leg were black as tar. I smiled at Mrs. Shackleford, who was stirring a huge battered pot on the stove.

She blew on a spoonful of chili, offered me a taste, then tucked her hands into the rear pockets of her jeans and waited for my verdict.

The chili was rich with garlic and onions, but there was no blue-flame kick from jalapeño peppers.

"Does it need anything?" she asked.

"To be eaten."

"I guess that means it's good," she said, plopping the spoon back into the pot.

I sat Ellie in her high chair and gave her a cracker, then moseyed over for a peek at the porch-turned-bedroom.

Barnboard paneling on the walls. Speckled linoleum on the floor. A slightly swaybacked double bed, flanked by a rocking chair and a chest of drawers. Through the plain white curtains, a dim glow from McDonald's brightened the colors on a faded patchwork quilt. The simplicity of the room appealed to me and made me think of the farmhouse.

"I love it," I said, "and I'll take a quilt any day over a pink satin coverlet that won't stay on the bed."

Avanelle grinned at me over a stack of mismatched bowls, but her mother's attention was on Birdie who, with much scraping and groaning, was dragging the vanity stool into the kitchen.

"What are you doing?"

Birdie positioned the stool at the table, sat herself down, and said smugly, "I've got a secret, and I've got a seat."

". . . and thank you, God," prayed Birdie, "for Velveeta's Aunt Queenie. You know her from church—the lady with the bird nest on her head. Amen."

Aunt Queenie? What brought that up? I stared at Birdie, bobbing on her stool like a cork in rough water.

"Okay, Birdie," said her mother as she ladled up a bowl of chili. "Get it out of your system. Tell Delrita the secret."

"My daddy's got a job!"

If I hadn't already been standing, I'd have leaped to my feet. "No kidding?" I said to Mr. Shackleford. "You found a job?"

The haunted look in his eyes was gone. "Actually, the job found me," he said. "The director of the nursing home came by today and offered it to me. Seems their maintenance man can't keep up with all the painting and repairs, so they need a second pair of hands. I start Monday."

"Wow."

"The credit goes to a certain member of the advisory board—your aunt Queenie. Evidently, the board's been haggling over hiring a second man for quite a while, and your aunt told them it was time for action. She gave them my name. Said she'd vouch for me."

"Chances are, she just wore them out," I said. "Aunt Queenie's not one to take 'no' for an answer."

"Well, I'm grateful." Mr. Shackleford rubbed his jaw and added, "I'm still not sure why she'd risk her reputation for me."

"Queenie knows you were innocent of that crime," said his wife. "Besides, she strikes me as a person who'd give any man a second chance."

Not necessarily, I thought, knowing the fur would fly if she caught Mr. Roebuck spitting in her dieffenbachia again.

"Hey, sis," said Tree, "what'll you take to wash the dishes?"

"What'll you give?" asked Avanelle.

"Half of what I earned at Coach's house this afternoon."

"Very funny."

"I know. I'm a riot. So will you wash the dishes, or not? A bunch of us guys are gonna watch a weight-lifting video at Todd's."

Tree was *leaving?* I studied the cracker crumbs on the table, hoping no one would see my disappointment.

"Go ahead," said Avanelle, "but don't forget you owe me. Big time."

"Thanks, sis. For a wart, you're all right."

As it turned out, though, Avanelle and her mom herded the younger kids into the tub while her dad and I cleaned up the kitchen. We didn't talk much. It was too hard to hear over the squealing and splashing and complaining coming from the bathroom. When the kids had been read to and tucked into bed, Mr. Shackleford challenged us ladies to a game of pitch.

"I'm not sure I have the strength to lift the cards," said his wife, frowning at the pile of dirty clothes outside the bathroom door. It looked like a week's worth to me.

"Come on, Mom," coaxed Avanelle. "We need four people."

"All right, but only if I'm not partners with your dad. He plays for blood, and I don't have any to spare."

"I'll be your partner," said Avanelle.

"Uh-oh," I said, glancing at Mr. Shackleford. "Where does that leave me?"

His answer was to grin and make his caterpillar eyebrows do pushups.

That worried me, but I soon figured out his bark was worse than his bite. He pounded on the table and yelled a lot, regardless of whether we won a round or lost it. I was flabbergasted that a person could get so worked up over a simple game of cards.

Near the end of the third game, both teams were neck-and-neck when I saved his trey with a ten.

"Way to go!" he hooted. "Delrita, you put us over the top!"

"Let me guess, Dad," said a voice from the doorway. "You won again."

Tree was back. I looked at him leaning against the doorpost, and I looked at the clock by his head. Almost ten-thirty. It seemed impossible, but I hadn't even thought about him for two hours.

"He won," said his mother, pushing herself up from her chair, "and here's one tired mama who's heading for bed."

"Don't let me break up the party," Tree said.

"You're not. It's been a long day."

"That it has," said Mr. Shackleford. With a wink at Avanelle, he slipped around behind his wife and nuzzled the back of her neck.

"Trezane, stop that!" She pulled away from him, blushing furiously, then said, "Good night, kids," and escaped into the new bedroom.

"Ditto," said Mr. Shackleford. Chuckling to himself, he followed her and closed the door.

"Dad used to do that to Mom," I said. "He'd get all lovey-dovey and she'd get so embarrassed. I miss it. Can you see Uncle Bert nuzzling Aunt Queenie?"

Tree sat down in his father's chair and gathered up the cards. "Never happen."

Avanelle snorted. "What makes you such an expert on romance?"

"I won't mention any names," he said, casually shuffling the deck, "but I have been compared to a Hershey's Kiss."

My pulse shot up to lickety-split.

"Puh-lease," said Avanelle.

Was he teasing me, or flirting? I would never know, because I didn't have the nerve to look at his face. I could only stare at his freckled hands flipping those cards.

"I'll stand you girls in a game of nurtz," he said.

Acting ever so cool, I hooked a strand of hair behind my ear and said, "You're on." Nurtz called for two decks of cards, and you had to be quick on the trigger. No problem. I was feeling wired.

Although Avanelle and I gave it our best shot, we were no match for Tree. By one o'clock, we were twenty-eight points behind.

"I've had enough," she said.

My nerves were jangling and my vision was blurry from the breakneck speed of the game, but I wasn't ready to give up this time with Tree. "But he's ahead," I said.

"I don't care," she insisted, standing up. "I quit."

Tree jabbed a finger at his cheek. "Put 'er there, sis. Kiss a champ good night."

"Right. So I can puke up two bowls of chili."

Laughing, Tree headed off to bed.

I changed clothes and brushed my teeth while Avanelle made a bed for herself on the couch. While she was taking her turn in the bathroom, I unrolled my sleeping bag on the floor and climbed in.

When she was settled under her covers, I said, "Want to hear a secret? It's not as good as Birdie's."

"Sure," she murmured, eyes already closed.

I told her about Mr. Roebuck's tape recording and why it was hush-hush.

"Well, now he's got a broken leg," she said drowsily, "so your aunt Queenie can't pester him to go to that reunion."

"But she could pester him to write the book. I wonder if she knows he spent three days on a mattress with a dead man?"

"Sweet dreams to you, too," she said, turning out the light.

16

A Whopper
of a Secret

I emerged from sleep slowly, reluctant to let go of my dream. Like stereo, I could hear two sets of voices—my parents talking in the dream and in the kitchen.

I snuggled down into my sleeping bag, comforted by the murmur of their conversation. Other sounds crept into my consciousness. The whoosh of water as Mom filled the coffeepot. The burbling of the coffeemaker. Dad rustling the pages of the newspaper.

Then I heard quiet laughter—too rumbling to be Dad and too tinkling to be Mom—and I remembered. My parents were dead.

Reality. A knife in my chest. I opened my eyes, and there was Avanelle asleep on the couch. The sleeping bag no longer felt snug, but confining. I unzipped it and kicked myself free.

From the girls' bedroom came a loud, scraping sound that

brought Mrs. Shackleford out of the kitchen. She shot past me, saying, "Birdie, you put that stool right back where you found it."

"Ellie wants out of her crib."

"Not if she's going to land on her head."

I lifted up enough to see tiny legs bicycling air. Mrs. Shackleford, still in her nightgown, was changing Ellie's diaper. Soon she sailed past me again, carrying the baby.

I turned onto my side and stared at the red crayon scribbles on the front door. When someone knocked, I sat up with a jerk.

"Mmmph, what time is it?" groaned Avanelle.

I was squinting at my watch when Mr. Shackleford said, "Too early for good news," and stepped over me in his sock feet.

My first thought was that Uncle Bert and Aunt Queenie had been in an accident. But that couldn't be right. Who would know to look for me here?

Mr. Shackleford opened the door to a man in uniform.

"Trezane Shackleford?"

"That's me," he said as he rolled up a sleeve on his chambray shirt.

"I'm Sergeant Nolan Rybarger, Tangle Nook Police. We'd like you to come down to the station."

"Daddy?" whispered Birdie, who had slipped into the room and was clinging to her father's leg.

"It's all right, hon," he said, patting her on the back. "What's the problem, officer?"

"You'll find out down at the station."

"Who is it, Trez—?" said Mrs. Shackleford from the kitchen doorway. She ran out of words when she saw the policeman.

"Sergeant, can't you just tell me what this is about?"

"At the station."

"Please, Daddy," pleaded Birdie. "Don't go."

Mr. Shackleford kept his hand on her shoulder as he stared at the policeman. "Don't I have the right to know why?"

The man cast a doubtful look at Birdie. Finally, he said, "It's about the burglaries in Tangle Nook."

"You can't mean I'm a suspect? I—I've been playing by the rules."

"My orders are to take you to the station."

"Okay. Give me a minute." Mr. Shackleford closed the door. His face had drained of color, and he had a caged-animal look in his eyes when he spoke to his wife. "Gardenia, I don't know what's happening here, but I've got to go down to the station. It shouldn't take long."

"Mr. Police Man!" Birdie yelled to the door. "You can't take my daddy to jail! He's got a *job!*"

Without a word, Mr. Shackleford gently pried her loose from his leg and passed her to her mother.

Avanelle had risen from the couch, and Tree and Randolph had materialized in their bedroom doorway. Their faces were white as milk glass, and their green eyes registered fear.

"There's noth—" began Mr. Shackleford, but he had to stop and clear his throat. "There's nothing to worry about, because I haven't done anything wrong. I'll find out what's going on, and I'll be home before Mama can fix breakfast. Now I know this is an impossible question, but has anybody seen my shoes?"

In the bathroom, I rinsed my face with a threadbare washcloth and ran a comb through my hair. Still wearing the jogging suit I'd slept in, I opened the door and stepped into the kitchen.

It was like stepping onto a stage with characters who'd forgotten their lines. Birdie was twisting her shirttail. Tree was kneading Randolph's shoulders. Ellie was squirming in Avanelle's arms. All were staring at their mother's back, and she was staring at the stove.

A minute passed, then two.

Mrs. Shackleford pulled a big iron skillet from the oven, carried it to the table, and sank into a chair. "I can't do it," she said, and I thought she was talking about breakfast. She scraped at an invisible speck on the skillet with a thumbnail. "I can't go through it again. Kids to feed. Bills to pay. Decisions to make."

"It'll be okay, Mom," said Tree with a worried glance at Avanelle.

His mother seemed oblivious to him. To us all. "Why take him to the station?" she said. "He had nothing to do with those burglaries. It's not right to target a man just because he's on parole."

Tree lifted the skillet from her hands. "Take it easy, Mom. I'll brew up some French toast and feed the kids."

"I'll help," I said.

"Come on, Birdie," said Avanelle. "You can help me dress Ellie."

Birdie sniffed the air and wrinkled her nose. "Uh-uh. She's got a dirty diaper. I'll just wake up the boys, 'cause they really like French toast."

Mrs. Shackleford sat hunched over, hugging her elbows and staring off into space while Tree and I made a towering batch of toast.

Under ordinary circumstances, the toast would have disappeared in nothing flat, but these weren't ordinary circumstances. Out of eight kids, only Ellie, Gordy, and Eddie had healthy appetites, and Mrs. Shackleford didn't eat at all.

Avanelle was swabbing syrup out of Ellie's hair when we heard the front door open.

"I'm home," called Mr. Shackleford, and everyone old enough to understand what was going on heaved a sigh of relief.

When he strode into the kitchen, Mrs. Shackleford said, "Trezane?" as if he were an apparition. "What—what happened?"

"Being on parole evidently makes me a suspect for everything that comes down the pike. The police wanted to know where I was the nights those burglaries occurred."

"You've been right here with me and the kids every night since—" Mrs. Shackleford blanched and sank deeper into her chair. "I forgot about your meetings."

"Come on, hon. Take it easy. The police are fishing, that's all. They don't have any concrete evidence against me, I've reported regularly to my parole officer, and I've landed a job." Mr. Shackleford walked over behind his wife and massaged her shoulders. "I'm more worried about the job than the police at this point. The advisory board has to protect the integrity of the nursing home. If they find out about the police questioning me this morning, they could decide I'm not the man for them."

"What—what can we do?" whispered Mrs. Shackleford.

"Pray," he said.

"I've been doing plenty of that," she murmured.

"So have I."

Still hugging her elbows, Mrs. Shackleford glanced around the table at all the kids' faces. Finally, she stopped at mine. "Delrita," she said in a quavery voice, "will you run over to McDonald's and call Bert and Queenie? Tell them not to worry about picking all of us up for church."

"We're missing *church?*" asked Avanelle, the last word coming out in a squeal.

Mrs. Shackleford turned glistening eyes to her. "You bigger kids can go, but Bert and Queenie won't need to bring two cars. Queenie might want to go straight to the hospital, and besides, I feel weak as a cat."

Mr. Shackleford squatted down and peered into his wife's face, his caterpillar eyebrows a long, unbroken line. "Are you okay, hon?"

She closed her eyes, and two tears leaked out. "I will be after a while, but for now, I don't have the strength to leave this house. The Lord will understand."

But I didn't understand, and I thought Mrs. Shackleford was overreacting. It seemed to me that the police would naturally want to question a person on parole. Mr. Shackleford had been questioned and released, so what was the problem now?

At McDonald's, I dropped a quarter into the pay phone and dialed our number.

Uncle Bert answered on the fifth ring, just before the machine would have given me my own message. " 'Lo," he mumbled.

"Uncle Bert, sorry to wake you."

"That's okay, hon. I've been up once, but I dozed off again after Queenie called."

"She stayed at the hospital?"

"Yes. Wouldn't leave her dad. Thought she should be there this morning when the doctor comes in. Poor old Orvis has a pin in his hip and one in his leg, so his wings are clipped for a good long time."

"I'm really sorry," I said, thinking how ironic it was that Mr. Roebuck had mended my swan's wing before falling and clipping his own.

After I filled Uncle Bert in on what had transpired at the Shacklefords', he said, "Boy, when it rains, it pours."

For the first time, I noticed it wasn't raining, and the sun was bright. "You won't need to pick anyone up for church this morning," I said. "Tree, Avanelle, and I are the only ones going, and we can walk."

"Then I'll head for the hospital, as soon as I get dressed. Why don't you come with me? I hate leaving you alone again today."

"I'll be okay. You just go see about Aunt Queenie and her dad."

. . .

I found Avanelle in her bedroom, dressed in the black stirrup pants and a monstrous blue sweater that struck her mid-thigh. Her hair was slightly damp, as if she'd run a wet comb through it, and even that dab of water made it hang in fiery ringlets.

"You got ready fast," I said.

"Not fast enough for Tree. He practically beat down the bathroom door."

One bathroom for nine people. Until this moment, I hadn't really appreciated having my own private bathroom at Uncle Bert and Aunt Queenie's. My shampoo was in the backpack, and I decided to leave it there. I could get by if I wore my hair in a ponytail.

"You're next in line," said Avanelle, handing me the backpack.

"I washed already. I don't need the bathroom just to change clothes."

"If you're sure."

I pulled the door shut for privacy—and to muffle the argument starting in the living room. Randolph was accusing Birdie of hiding his cowboy boots.

Avanelle folded the blankets in the crib while I changed into teal-colored slacks and matching sweater. When I sat down on the vanity stool to brush my hair, she was making the bed. Eyeing her reflection, I said, "I really like your dresser."

Her face lit up for the first time that morning. "Slim—some guy Dad knows—hauled it over here in his pickup while we were at the birthday—" Abruptly, she stopped talking and sat on the bed as if she were a puppet and someone had dropped her strings.

I spun around on the stool. "What's the matter?"

"The rain," she said. "It was pouring rain."

What was she getting at? Her hands were trembling, and her face was chalky white.

"You can't move furniture in the rain, unless your pickup has a camper shell," she said.

"So? What's wrong with that?"

"The radio. Don't you listen to the radio? The police are looking for an old pickup with a camper shell."

"But you weren't even here to see the truck," I argued. "How do you know it's old?"

"I've seen it before. It's got a noisy engine, and you have to wire the tailgate shut."

"So your dad's got a friend who drives an old wreck of a rig. That's not a crime. I think you're seeing monsters in the closet."

"And the monster may be Slim. None of us know that much about him—what he's done or where he's been. I do know that Dad has this—this *habit* of choosing the wrong friends."

My scalp tingled. I didn't like the way this conversation was going.

"Slim was a total stranger, but his truck left him stranded at the grocery store a couple of weeks ago. Dad loaned him the battery out of the station wagon, and then had to walk home himself. Mom was mad. Said he'd probably never get the battery back."

"Did he?"

"Yeah, he did. Surprise, surprise."

"Doesn't that prove Slim's an honest man?"

"No, it just shows he appreciates a little help when he's down on his luck. Delrita, I—I'm really scared. What if Slim's the one who's been breaking into houses? What if the police know he's been over here a few times, buddying up to Dad? They had a reason for questioning Dad this morning. Maybe it's guilt by association. You know—choosing the wrong friends."

"But they let him go."

"For now. Who knows what'll happen next? The radio said they were looking for a burly man. Dad fits the description, and he's on parole. The police won't see Dad as a person, but as a man with a criminal record."

"He served his time."

"But he'll always have the criminal record. That's what's got me worried." Avanelle mashed a fist against her lips and stared at the floor, then lowered her hand and looked at me. "Remember the first time we ate lunch together at school? We talked about families having secrets."

I nodded. The discussion had been about Punky, and how I'd tried to keep him hidden from the world.

Avanelle's eyes, dark with pain, bored into mine. "Well," she said, "our family has a whopper of a secret that could ruin everything, and that's a part of the story you don't know. . . . Not even Tree has blabbed this secret. We—we're so ashamed. We've never told a soul."

17

A Little Seed
of Doubt

I could hear the blood pounding in my ears.
What dreadful secret was Avanelle about to reveal?

She traced a pattern on the quilt with a finger. "Mom's
really out of it today. She doesn't usually let them fight like
that."

It took a moment for me to realize she meant Birdie and
Randolph, still disagreeing over the boots. I nodded, im-
patient to hear the secret.

She traced the block again.

If I were a cat, curiosity would have cost me one of my
lives. I fidgeted on the vanity stool. It creaked and groaned,
probably the same as Miss Myrtle's old bones when she sat
on it.

Avanelle finally stopped tracing and looked me in the eye.
"Dad's been in prison *twice.*"

My brain didn't want to process that information. She

couldn't mean *the* Mr. Shackleford, who wrestled with his kids and made the caterpillars walk.

"I'm seven years older than Randolph," she said. "Haven't you ever wondered about the difference in our ages?"

"I—well—yes."

"When I was just a baby, Mom kicked Dad out of the house. He was drinking too much and got fired from two jobs. He was a real party animal—barhopping and running with a bunch of good-for-nothing friends. Then he got hired—" Avanelle ran a hand across her mouth, erasing the words, then squeezed her eyes shut and started over. "He got hired as an errand boy and chauffeur for a big-shot bar owner. Louie Gigliardo, a gangster."

I didn't move a muscle. I couldn't. The French toast was a slab of concrete in my stomach.

"One night, the police raided the bar and discovered a casino in the back room."

"Gambling?" I whispered.

"Yeah." Avanelle heaved a sigh so deep, it must have come up from her toes. "It's weird, isn't it? Gambling's legal in Missouri now, but it wasn't then. Louie and Dad and a few other guys ended up in prison. Louie's crime was gambling and tax evasion. Dad's crime was that he wouldn't talk about Louie to the grand jury. A prosecutor can't use grand jury evidence against you, but you *have* to testify. Dad went to prison for almost a year because he refused to testify against his boss. Louie threatened to have the family killed if he did."

I clenched my hands and looked at them, at a loss as to how to respond.

"In prison, Dad joined Alcoholics Anonymous," Avanelle said in a monotone. "When he got out, he went to work for the railroad, and Mom eventually took him back."

A little seed of doubt was sprouting in my mind. Mr. Shackleford had once run errands for a gangster, and now his family's funds were tight. Suppose he *was* involved in breaking into houses . . . But I was being disloyal to Avanelle. With an effort, I dragged my attention back to her.

". . . kicked the alcohol," she was saying, "but he still has this habit of choosing the wrong friends."

"Why? When he's still got the family to think about?"

Avanelle shrugged. "It just happens. Mom says Dad's worse than a kid for picking up strays. It's like he's trying to make it up to the whole world for his mistakes. Trying to change the past."

But he could never do that. Nobody knew that better than I.

"He'll believe any sob story," Avanelle said, "help anybody with any problem. You know that's what sent him to prison the last time. He stole a whole houseful of furniture, thinking he was helping some guys *move*." At the last word, her face crumpled slowly, like melting wax.

I wanted to cry for her. She'd been suffering her whole life over situations she couldn't control. Feeling as creaky as Miss Myrtle, I moved off the stool, sat on the bed, and laid my hand on her shoulder. It was small comfort, I know, but my brain had stalled. I couldn't think of a thing to say that wouldn't make her feel worse.

Tree, wearing jeans and a starched white shirt, was leaning against the cabinet, cleaning his fingernails with a pocketknife. His parents were slumped in their chairs, staring vacantly at coffee cups on the table. No one was talking, but worry charged the room like an electric current.

When Tree saw Avanelle and me, he closed the knife with a snap.

His mother jumped, then smiled weakly and fiddled with the neck of her wrinkled cotton dress.

My heart ached for her, for the times she'd carried the load by herself—and because she might have to do it again.

"You'll ask the folks at church to pray for us?" she said.

"If we ever get there," said Tree. He scowled at Avanelle. "Slowpoke. A herd of snails could move faster than you."

"Easy, son," said Mr. Shackleford, rubbing his red-rimmed eyes. "No sense compounding troubles with harsh words to each other."

"Sorry," mumbled Tree.

I walked over and touched his mother on the arm. "Thanks for letting me spend the night. I would have been climbing the walls at home."

Dumb choice of words. Climbing the walls. They shoot you for that in prison.

18

Seeing Ghosts

Shouldering my backpack, I stepped outside and blinked against the sunlight. Rainwater lay in shiny puddles on the Shacklefords' sidewalk, reflecting fluffy clouds and azure sky. The breeze carried the scent of warm mud, as though Mother Nature had seen all the holes in the yard and decided to bake mud pies.

I eased myself between Tree and Avanelle. Glum-faced and mum, we walked along Magnolia Street.

A woman in a bathrobe scuttled onto her porch and grabbed her Sunday paper. A collie sniffed at the base of a tree before lifting his leg and leaving his mark. A robin chirped.

"We could take a hint from the robin and cheer up, cheer up," said Tree with a tone that was anything but cheerful.

Staring straight ahead, Avanelle said, "Tree, Delrita knows the whole story. I told her all of it—about Dad's drinking and getting mixed up with that gangster and going to prison."

"Hmmmpf," he grunted. "Seems to me you're the one who's always talking about telephone, television, and tell-a-Tree."

"I know. But Delrita heard those reports on the radio, and she was there when the policeman came."

"Pardon me," I said, "but you guys are acting like I'm not even here."

Tree cast a sidelong glance at me, rammed his hands into the pockets of his jeans, and kicked a stone off the sidewalk. "So are we still friends?"

"Why wouldn't we be?"

"Because now you know the Shacklefords' deep, dark past. We've been through some pretty stormy situations."

"But I'm not a fair-weather friend."

Tree tweaked my ponytail, then dropped his hand to the back of my neck and squeezed. "Not just plain Velveeta," he said.

"Huh?"

"You're that spicy kind with the jalapeño peppers."

Instantly, I felt a burning where Tree's hand had touched my neck, and I thought of Dad's blue flame chili, guaranteed to set you on fire.

Countryside Church sat between a hayfield and a cornfield just outside of town. Because the building was so tiny, the two dozen cars in the parking lot meant a full house. We'd missed Sunday school, but were in plenty of time for church.

After the song service, Brother Hicks, our minister, gave a rundown of people on the prayer list, including Orvis Roebuck. Peering out at the congregation, he asked, "Are there other needs we should pray about this morning?"

Two women added names to the list, but Tree whispered to me, "I'm gonna do more than just give Dad's name. I don't want to be a fair-weather son."

"What?" I whispered back, but he was already on his feet.

Ears turning red, he faced the crowd. "Y'all know," he began in a cracking voice that soon leveled off, "my dad's had a hard time finding a job since he got out of prison. He's supposed to start work tomorrow at Rest Haven Nursing Home, but that could fall through if the board finds out the police questioned him this morning about the burglaries in Tangle Nook."

Gasps and murmurs rippled across the room. Avanelle was clenching her hands and breathing hard. I could understand her embarrassment, but at the same time, I admired her brother's courage.

The sanctuary grew quiet. Tree filled his lungs with air and plunged on: "The police are on the wrong track. How can I be sure of that? Two reasons—my father is a changed man, and my mother is a Christian woman. She's brought all of us kids to church every Sunday, and lately she's been bringing Dad, too. She kicked him out of the house a long time ago when she disapproved of his lifestyle, and she'd do it again before she'd live with a thief. So please, y'all, just pray for Dad. For the whole family."

Tree dropped down beside me, his breath whooshing out

and his big hands trembling violently. "It's a lot easier being Outrageous," he hissed.

I leaned close to his ear. "You should be a lawyer. If the church was a courtroom, and I was on the jury, I'd vote your dad 'not guilty.' "

"I couldn't have done it without my all-weather friend," he said, catching my hand between both of his.

We sat that way through the sermon, and not one word of it sank in.

After the service, a crowd gathered around Tree and Avanelle to offer support. I stood by quietly, but I wanted to skip and sing. Believing in Mr. Shackleford's innocence had taken a load off my mind.

When we finally left the church, Avanelle punched Tree on the arm and muttered, "I wish Mom would either tie you to a bedpost or sew your lips shut. You just can't keep a secret."

"Give it a rest, sis. You told Velveeta the whole story."

"That's different. Why couldn't you have just asked folks to pray for Dad and left it at that? This *is* Tangle Nook, Missouri, you know."

"So?"

"So it's the gossip capital of the world. That's how it got its name."

"You're joshing me."

"No, she's not," I said, grabbing my chance to jump into the conversation. "There used to be nothing here but a crossroads and a trading post. The post was a stagecoach stop on the Butterfield Line. It's where settlers got their news—from other settlers and from folks just passing through. Some of the news was just plain gossip. Stories got tangled, reputations got ruined, and one man even got shot. So the Butterfield drivers started calling this place 'Tangle Nook.'"

"How'd you know all that?" Tree asked.

"Some old records Dad found in a desk."

"So you see, Trezane," said Avanelle, "you'd better watch your mouth."

We parted ways at the next intersection. I saw that Fain's Drugstore was having a sale on nail polish, so I moseyed in.

Drat! Sophie Breech was cruising toward me in the makeup aisle. Draped over her shoulders was a fox stole—real, not fake, with the fox's head and tail still attached.

That seemed appropriate for Sophie Breech, who had a cruel streak a mile long. She was the town's biggest gossip, and from her mouth came poison darts.

Once, when Aunt Queenie was hosting the garden club, Mrs. Breech cornered me in the kitchen, expressed sorrow at my parents' death, then asked me if the funeral service had been closed casket. I'd gone speechless with anger.

Even now, I was furious just thinking about it. I turned away from her, hid behind the backpack, and stared unseeingly at the nail polish display. Which color should I buy? Puky purple? Ridiculous Red? P.U. Pink?

"Delrita! Hello!"

I grunted a response. Don't look at her, I told myself. Don't give the old busybody an opening.

"How's Queenie's father doing? I heard about his fall."

"He's alive," I mumbled to a bottle on the shelf. "That's all I know."

"Did Queenie spend the night at the hospital?"

"Yeah."

"She would. The poor thing has such a sense of obligation."

"Well, he *is* her father," I said, turning around in spite of myself. The woman's narrow face was amazingly like the fox's, with its long, pointy nose and beady eyes.

"Can't turn your back on your father," she twittered, *"or* an orphaned niece. Queenie doesn't complain, of course, but I've noticed a difference in her lately. So many responsibilities. She's quieter, more preoccupied, and she's starting to show her age."

You should talk, I fumed, staring at the makeup caked in the gullies of her face.

Mrs. Breech flashed her sharp little teeth. "But what can you expect? What Queenie's going through would have an adverse effect on anybody. For years, it was just her and Bert, and then in the span of a few short months, she wound up with a teenager and an aging parent on her doorstep."

"You make us sound like charity cases," I said hotly. "We're not."

"I'm not implying anything of the sort. I'm saying only that Queenie Holloway is not the type to leave you hanging. She may not want the responsibilities, but she'll shoulder them with a smile on her face. That's just her nature. Please tell her that I asked about her father." With that, Sophie Breech swooped away.

I stood rooted to the spot, my heart beating so hard and fast it hurt. Consider the source, I told myself. That woman is shallow, obnoxious, two bricks shy of a load.

Nail polish forgotten, I aimed for the door. There was Sophie Breech in a checkout lane, reading *The National Enquirer*. A sensational, front-page headline flashed across my mind: WOMAN STRANGLED WITH HER OWN FOX STOLE.

What happened next was so out of character for me, I still can't believe I did it. I deliberately made myself the center of attention. "Excuse me . . . Excuse me," I said as I squeezed past the people in line. When I reached Mrs. Breech, I crowded her with my backpack. "Yo, Soph."

"Yes?"

I tapped the tabloid. "Get a life."

"How rude!" she gasped, her face turning red and her eyes flitting toward the customers around us.

Her discomfort didn't make up for the poison darts, but it helped. I patted the fox's head, said, "See you around, big guy," and marched out of the store.

At home, I opened all the drapes and turned the stereo up loud, then popped some leftovers in the microwave. I smiled at the Sunday paper scattered across the table. Uncle Bert had seized the opportunity to read it over breakfast. With Aunt Queenie gone, I could read it over lunch.

While eating carrots, potatoes, and pot roast, I scanned the front page of the paper for a report on the burglaries. Nothing. Just people in big cities, killing each other. On page two, births and deaths, marriage and divorce, canceling each other out. Page three, editorials. On page four, a full-color ad caught my eye: "Coming to the Regency Auditorium, Friday night, April 23rd. *CIRCUS VEGAS!* TIGERS! ELEPHANTS! ACROBATS! CLOWNS! TRAPEZE ARTISTS!"

Tree would love the circus, would love watching the professional clowns at work. But when I saw the ticket prices, I knew he wouldn't go. No way would he buy a ticket for himself and leave his brothers and sisters at home.

After lunch, I headed in to clean my closet to satisfy Aunt Queenie. As soon as I smelled the cedar, I thought of Orvis Roebuck's closet and the helmets in his duffel bag. Then I thought of the swan he'd rescued from my wastebasket, and the blanks he'd cut for me. A grouch with a soft side. No wonder he needed two helmets.

My closet was a walk-in, like the one I'd had at home, but this one didn't have shelves. I'd used those shelves to stash books and my Barbie case. What was Heidi storing there? Sweaters? Games? Art supplies?

Probably art supplies. I remembered her watercolor painting of the woman squinting at the sky. The girl was talented in art—no question about that. So let her use some of that talent to teach herself to carve.

Agitated, I shoved the garments on the rod as far to the right as they would go. That brought into full view the navy blue dress I'd worn to my parents' funeral. Tears sprang to my eyes, and I yanked the dress off its hanger and tossed it to the floor.

Hanger by hanger, I sorted through my clothes and weeded out a good-sized stack of giveaways. The last pieces to go were the mint-green dress with the flounces on the skirt, and the "Tightwad" T-shirt. Both were too small for me now, but Mom had really liked those flounces, and Dad had bought the shirt as a joke from the bank in Tightwad, Missouri. . . .

Aching with memories, I packed everything neatly in a box and closed the lid. Closed off another little part of my past. Suddenly, I needed to hold my carving tools in my hands, feel the basswood yield under my control.

I escaped to the family room and retrieved the Barbie case from behind the couch. The new project didn't look much like a bear yet, but as I laid out my tools, I let my thoughts leap ahead. I'd use walnut stain on the body. Red and black paint for the plaid on the paws. Pink for the nose and mouth. Black for the eyes. No. *One* eye, like the real Peanut.

I had no trouble roughing in the bear's head, but when it was time to detail the facial features, I tapped my knife against my chin. What, exactly, does a teddy bear's snout look like? Where does the mouth begin?

What I needed was another bear to go by, but I'd given all my stuffed animals to Toys for Tots. I wondered again about Mom's old teddy bear. Where was it now?

I was still wondering when I heard the kitchen door open, heard Uncle Bert call, "Delrita? I'm home."

"Coming." I brushed wood shavings off my lap, then went in to meet him with the carving in my hand. "Hi. How's Mr. Roebuck?"

"Grumpy, as usual." He dropped onto a chair, plucked

off his toupee, and tossed it on the table. "The doctor said it's a miracle, but there's no sign of pneumonia."

"Where's Aunt Queenie?"

"A few minutes behind me. She stopped at the grocery store."

"Then you're living dangerously," I said, and stashed the toupee in the closet.

Uncle Bert grinned when I sat across from him. "Thanks, although at this point, a little hair on the table wouldn't bother Queenie a bit."

"Why not?"

"Orvis has been a holy terror all day. He'll be laid up for a while, and the doctor thinks he should recuperate in the nursing home."

"Oooh-boy."

"Orvis wanted Queenie to take care of him here, but I set my foot down on that. She's not strong enough to do the necessary lifting, and he'll get good care at the nursing home. Besides, he was hard to get along with before, and he'd drive her crazy now. She can visit him whenever she wants to, but I won't have her becoming his slave."

"She went along with that?" I asked, incredulous.

"To tell the truth, I think she was relieved. How about you? How'd you get along while we were gone?"

"Okay. I had fun last night at the Shacklefords'. Went to church this morning, cleaned out my closet, and I've been carving for the last couple of hours. . . . Uncle Bert, do you remember Mom's old teddy bear? The one she got when she was a little girl?"

"Bruno. The folks gave him to her when I was born."

"Bruno?"

"Yep. She slept with him for years." He chuckled, and his eyes took on a faraway look. "I was five years old when I got a cowboy outfit and a badge for Christmas. I also got a licking, because I took Bruno out to the barn and hung him for stealing my horse." Uncle Bert chuckled again at the memory, then sobered and said, "Whatever made you ask about that old bear?"

I showed him the carving. "Joey's is just like Mom's, and having hers to go by would help me get the face right. I remember her bear in the rocking chair at the farmhouse, but I never saw it after we moved to town."

"Sorry, hon," said Uncle Bert, shaking his head. "Can't say as I know where it would be now."

"The house here was a lot smaller than the farmhouse, so maybe Mom packed Bruno away in the cedar chest or someplace. Is it possible that you—uh—shipped him out with her and Dad's other stuff?"

"Delrita," he said softly, "I moved the antiques to the shop and sold the other furniture, because you were so adamant about it. But I didn't sell their personal things. They're stored in boxes in the garage. That was Queenie's idea. She figured someday you'd want them, after the pain goes away."

Would the pain ever go away? Somehow I didn't think so.

"We saved Sam's basketball trophies and scrapbooks from high school," Uncle Bert went on. "Shirley's old dollhouse.

Those pineapple lace doilies that she loved—that sort of thing—but I don't recall seeing that bear."

I felt a cold sweat on my brow. I remembered the musty smell of Dad's scrapbooks, the brown shoestring wrapped around the one with the broken binding. I remembered Mom's doilies on every stick of furniture. But I wasn't ready to touch those things or look at them. That would be like seeing ghosts.

Uncle Bert knelt beside my chair and put his arms around me. "I'm sorry, hon. Guess I should have kept my mouth shut."

"It's all right. I'm glad you saved their personal stuff. I just—I'm not ready to deal with it yet."

"Want me to dig around for old Bruno?" asked Uncle Bert as he smoothed the bangs off my forehead.

I nodded, then sat stiffly and listened while he rummaged through the boxes in the garage. I heard him talking to himself, and once I heard him sob. That's the first time I really thought about the huge responsibilities he'd been saddled with from the moment of my parents' death. Executor of their estate. Legal guardian to Punky and me. Funeral arrangements, twice. He'd had to deal with it all, in spite of his grief.

When he came back, his bald head was dusty, his face pale. "I didn't see anything, hon," he said, but I knew different. His haunted eyes told me he'd seen the ghost of Shirley Jensen—his sister and my mom.

19

On the
Hot Seat

"I'm home," sang Aunt Queenie as she walked in the back door, carrying a big white paper bag. She stopped short at the sight of Uncle Bert and me sitting morosely at the table. "Well, I declare. Why all the gloom?"

"Hi, hon." Uncle Bert got up and pecked her on the cheek. "We—uh—Delrita knows about the things in the garage."

"Oh?" she said, her eyes darting toward me.

I knew I should thank her, but I didn't trust myself to speak. I dropped my gaze to the bag and saw a spot turning gray with grease.

Uncle Bert explained to Aunt Queenie about Mom's Bruno Bear, then asked if she knew where it was. She didn't.

"Maybe it was tucked away in a dresser drawer and got sold with the furniture," she said.

"Maybe," sighed Uncle Bert. "I wouldn't have sold it on

purpose, but who knows? I had plenty of details to take care of." He ran a hand across his pate, noticed the dust, and headed for the sink.

"Maybe this will lighten everybody up," said Aunt Queenie, giving the bag an enticing shake.

"What is it?" Uncle Bert asked as he swiped at his head with a wet paper towel.

Aunt Queenie set the bag on the table, and a mouth-watering aroma seeped out. "Deli food. Fried chinny and potato salad."

I stared at her, doubly surprised. First, fried chicken was a no-no around here. And second, she'd used Punky's word "chinny" just as naturally as you please. She surprised me again when she arranged her purchases on the table. Not once in the seven months I'd lived here had we used paper plates and paper napkins.

Soon we were feasting on fat and cholesterol, and Aunt Queenie smiled at Uncle Bert. "I'm glad you're enjoying this. You certainly deserve a treat."

His forkful of potato salad halted in midair. "I do?"

"Yes, for standing up to Pop. You're right, you know. He'd have me running in circles if I tried to take care of him here."

"He'll keep you hopping between here and the nursing home, but at least it won't be twenty-four hours a day."

"I worked out a schedule on the drive home." Aunt Queenie plucked the pencil from her topknot, and made checkmarks on a napkin as she ticked off chores: "Tomorrow morning and Tuesday, I'll be visiting Pop at the hospital, so that means calling donors for the blood drive in the afternoons. He'll be transferred to Rest Haven Wednesday, so I'll drop by there when I leave the crisis center . . ."

I stopped listening. Aunt Queenie was organizing, which is what she did best, and she seemed almost happy that her father was out of the house.

Without warning, my brain conjured up one of Sophie Breech's poison darts: *"So many responsibilities. She's quieter, more preoccupied, and she's starting to show her age."*

I stared at Aunt Queenie. She didn't look older to me.

But would she be happier if *I* were out of the house? If she didn't have to attend school activities? Run me to the dentist? Drive me and my friends to a birthday party on a Saturday afternoon?

"She may not want the responsibilities," Sophie Breech had said, *"but she'll shoulder them with a smile on her face."*

"Delrita?"

I blinked at Uncle Bert. "What?"

He motioned to the remains of the chicken leg in my hand. "I asked if you were going to play Punky and fling that behind the TV."

"I'm sorry," I said, dropping the bone onto my plate. "I was thinking of something else."

"I know," replied Aunt Queenie. "You were a million miles away."

"And you weren't far behind her," said Uncle Bert as he pointed to the pencil on the table.

Aunt Queenie's hand flew to her head, where a chicken bone protruded from her topknot. "Well, I declare," she said, pulling out the bone, and all three of us burst out laughing.

Aunt Queenie had definitely been preoccupied, but that was understandable for a person who'd been sitting at the hospital all night. I pushed away thoughts of Sophie Breech. She was a shallow, obnoxious woman, and I refused to give credit to a word she said.

When our laughter died down, Aunt Queenie looked at Uncle Bert, shamefaced. "Well, I declare. We're carrying on like we don't have a care in the world, while Pop's hurt and Trezane Shackleford's got trouble with the police." Turning to me, she said, "I've had Gardenia on my mind since Bert told me this morning. How is she?"

"Worried sick," I said. "The whole family's upset. Mr. Shackleford's afraid the board'll decide they don't want him working at the nursing home."

"Not if I can help it," declared Aunt Queenie.

"Watch out, board," Uncle Bert said to the ceiling. "My wife's a formidable foe."

Aunt Queenie kept on talking as if she hadn't heard. "He didn't try to mislead anybody when he filled out the application. He wrote right on it that he'd served two terms in prison. I'll have to admit, that gave me pause, but we called him in for an interview, and he was straight with us."

"His family was at risk," said Uncle Bert. "Can't blame him for being afraid to testify."

I gaped at him in astonishment.

"Bert and I don't keep secrets from each other," said Aunt Queenie.

Uncle Bert leaned back in his chair and rubbed his paunch. "That family's had a rough row to hoe, that's for sure. Delrita, the Chamber of Commerce gave me a bunch of free tickets. How'd you like to take those kids to the circus?"

I wanted to plant a dozen kisses on his shiny head. Tree would get to see the clowns, after all. "Terrific! I'll take the Shacklefords and Joey, too."

"Delrita," said Aunt Queenie, "Mrs. Marcum is beginning to loosen her protective reins, but I doubt she'll let you take Joey to the circus."

"She let him go to the birthday party," I said.

"She knew he'd be with little kids. The circus is too big a step. You're talking a huge crowd, maybe hundreds of people."

"You could give her one of your pep talks," I persisted. "I'll bet she'd let him go if you went with us."

"I have absolutely no interest in seeing a circus."

"But you do have an interest in people like Joey. You're the reason Joey's got a job now. Mrs. Marcum told me so."

Aunt Queenie pursed her lips and looked thoughtful, and I knew she was wavering. I drew a deep breath and pulled out all the stops. "Aunt Queenie, you were the one who said Punky needed to expand his horizons in order to grow. You said Mom and I were smothering him with our protectiveness."

"I was talking about a job for him and self-esteem. You're talking about a fly-by-night circus. It's not the same thing."

"It's still a new experience, a new horizon. Think how Punky blossomed when he finally spread his wings."

Aunt Queenie picked up her pencil and tapped its eraser on the table. "Hmmmmm," she murmured. "I do have to fill out some papers for Pop at the nursing home tomorrow. I suppose I could drop in and have a little chat with Mrs. Marcum."

Uncle Bert and Aunt Queenie went to church that evening because they'd missed the morning service. I stayed home to do some assigned reading and to circle prepositions in my English workbook. To, for, of, between—little words, so unimportant.

When the phone rang, I almost let the machine pick up, and then I remembered its message was *about* the birdies *in* the trees. I dashed into the hall and snatched up the receiver. "Hello?"

"Who'm I talking to?" said Orvis Roebuck in a gargly voice. "Is that you, girlie?"

I heard him spitting, and I figured if they'd let him have a spit can, he couldn't be in too bad a shape. "Yes, it's me. Sorry about your accident. How are you?"

"I've been better. Where's Queen?"

"At church with Uncle Bert."

"Good. Then she won't have to know about this call. I need to ask a favor, and I hope it's not too late."

"I already hid your tape recorder." I tightened my grip on the receiver and told him the rest of it. "The safest place I could think of—in your duffel bag."

Several seconds passed with no sound but his wheezing. Was he going to chew me out for entering his room? For touching his precious duffel bag? Finally, he said, "Thanks. You saved my hide."

"You're welcome." The line was silent, except for the wheezing and a faint crackle of static. Without mentioning the nursing home, I couldn't think of anything intelligent to say.

"Girlie, I'm gonna be stuck in the old folks' home for a month or so."

"I heard. I'm sorry."

"I was wondering if you'd slip that recorder out of the house and bring it to me on the days Queen's gonna be tied up. I'd have to ask you to wait for it and take it back home when I'm done."

"You couldn't keep it in your room?"

"No. Queen's apt to find it, or somebody might steal it. That fellow they've hired just got out of prison."

"But he didn't steal—"

"So whadda you say, girlie? Will you bring me the recorder or not? It wouldn't be but a few days, just long enough for me to finish what I've started."

My brain kicked into overdrive, and I came up with a way to get what I needed without being a bother to him. "Tell you what, Mr. Roebuck. I'm supposed to interview a combat veteran and write a report for history class. If I wrote about you, we wouldn't have to do an actual interview. I could just listen to your tapes."

"Absolutely not," he sputtered, like an engine that's blown a gasket. "Those are my private thoughts about the war."

"You want the tape recorder, but you don't want to deal. Is that fair?"

"Girlie, you don't understand," Mr. Roebuck said. "These stories I'm telling are ugly. They're not fit for a little girl to hear."

"I know horrible things happened during the war, but I'm tougher than you think."

More silence. More static. Mr. Roebuck was weighing his options.

I remembered the Uncle Sam poster hanging in his room and, as I had with Aunt Queenie, I pulled out all the stops. I told him the story Mrs. Bagby had told us about the infantryman on Guadalcanal. "Too many grownups think kids today don't have deep feelings about anything. All I can say is, they should have been in history class when nineteen of us heard why that dying man wanted the flag. They'd have seen the patriotism in that room."

"All right," he said at last. "You can play the tapes, but don't say I didn't warn you."

"Thanks, Mr. Roebuck."

"Just don't go turning that recorder on yet. There's a place or two where I should clean up the language."

A place or two? I pictured a smokestack belching pollution, fouling the air for miles around. I was smiling when I hung up the phone.

Before long, though, I was having second thoughts about cutting the deal with Mr. Roebuck. How could I listen to his tapes and still keep the secret from Aunt Queenie? Suppose I was playing them and she knocked on my door? Or suppose she or Uncle Bert passed by and his gravelly voice carried out into the hall?

I'd be in hot water. On the hot seat. Up the creek without a paddle. I stared glumly at my list of prepositions. I felt caught between the swatter and the fly.

20

Head Lice
and Headaches

The air was brisk, exhilarating, as I left my house Monday morning, but I noticed a definite strain in the atmosphere at Avanelle's. Fussy kids, fussy parents. My announcement about Uncle Bert's free circus tickets barely made a ripple.

"That's great, Velveeta," Tree said, but it sounded fake and he didn't crack a smile. When he left the house without Randolph, Avanelle griped until we were out the door ourselves.

As we walked to school, she kept yanking irritably at the too-short tail of her sweater and hollering at Randolph, who wouldn't wait up. The problem wasn't her brothers, I knew, but worry about her dad. His parting words before going to the nursing home had been, "Let's hope they don't send me right back."

They just might, too, if the board members were as hard-headed as Orvis Roebuck.

When I told Avanelle about the deal I'd made with him, she said, "Good. Now I can stop feeling like a blabbermouth."

After making sure Randolph reached the elementary school, we cut across the back way to the junior high. The wall was covered with kids again, and there sat Tree with Heidi Grissom.

"Look at that," said Avanelle. "Heidi's still hanging around with the ninth-graders. She's the only person our age on that wall."

I hadn't noticed that. I'd been too busy noticing Heidi's haircut and new earrings. Or maybe they were old earrings that had been hidden before by all the hair. Whatever. They were long, dangly silver things that reflected the sunlight with each bob of her head.

"Delrita and Avanelle. Hi!" she called.

"Hi," we answered with the enthusiasm of overcooked spaghetti.

I tried to act nonchalant, but I felt her and Tree watching me as we drew near to them.

"Velveeta," he said, "I was just telling Heidi about the circus tickets."

She nodded her blond head, and the earrings went berserk. "All those professional clowns," she gushed. "He should pick up lots of pointers."

Pointers. Right. Wish I could point her back to Arkansas. Wish I could point out to Tree that just a while ago, he'd been ho-hum about the tickets. His all-weather friend was feeling stormy, with the possibility of showers.

· · ·

At lunchtime, Heidi joined Avanelle and me at our table. That was a first, and it made me think she was trying to get on Avanelle's good side on account of Tree.

"Delrita," she said as she opened her milk carton, "I wanted you to know I found a combat veteran. Gramps asked his customers at the antique shop, and believe it or not, one old guy was a prisoner of war."

"That's nice," I replied, then thought how stupid that sounded. What could be nice about being a prisoner of war?

"Tree told me about Mr. Roebuck's accident," she said. "How's he doing?"

"Okay. He's grouchy, but he was that way before, so I can't tell much difference."

"I'm really sorry about Saturday. I asked you in front of your aunt if you intended to interview him. I got to thinking about it later, and I must have put you on the spot."

I shrugged. "Forget it. I've got it all worked out."

Avanelle stirred the glop on her tray. "What *is* this stuff?"

"In Arkansas, we called it goulash. You know—food for ghouls." Heidi opened her eyes wide, curled her hands like claws, and moaned, "I'm the Ghoul of Gotcha Goomy, and I need my goooooo-oulash."

Avanelle laughed so hard, she got the hiccups. I couldn't believe it. All the king's horses and all the king's men couldn't have dragged a smile out of her this morning.

That reminded me of the book of nursery rhymes Heidi had been toting at Rest Haven. Bet that girl was a riot with old people. "Heidi," I said, "how long have you been a Teen Buddy?"

Her ghoulish expression changed to a pout. She twiddled an earring. "I—uh—how long have I lived here? Three weeks? Yeah, that's it. Three weeks."

Aunt Queenie would love Heidi Grissom. No begging her to volunteer. She'd jumped in with both feet as soon as she hit Tangle Nook.

Avanelle's father still had a job Tuesday, so she wasn't down in the mouth anymore. At lunch, she talked about Miss Myrtle's adventures in Burma, and Heidi talked about Don Delgado, her prisoner of war.

"The men in the prison camps didn't have razors or anything, so they couldn't shave," Heidi said. "They had lice crawling in their hair and beards and eyebrows. To this day, Mr. Delgado feels itchy when he sees a man with a beard."

Why did she have to discuss lice at the lunch table? And when did Avanelle start thinking of Heidi Grissom as a friend?

I was jealous, plain and simple, and it didn't help that I had nothing to add to the conversation. I found myself wishing Mr. Roebuck was back in town, so he could clean up the language on his tape recordings.

He called from the hospital as soon as I got home from school. "Hello, girlie," he said. "Is it safe to talk?"

"I don't know. I just walked in the door."

"Check around, will you? See where Queen's at."

I did as he asked, then returned to the phone. "Her car's gone."

"Good. Tomorrow I get shipped to the old folks' home. Can you bring me that recorder after school?"

"On your first day?"

"All the days are gonna be the same in that place, what with everybody sittin' around waitin' to die. Besides, it'll be Wednesday, and Queen'll work late at the crisis center. If you don't bring it then, we might have to wait another week."

I couldn't wait that long. My report was due a week from Friday, and besides, I wanted stories of my own to tell at lunch. "Okay. I'll bring it."

"You'll hide it real good, won't you? So Queen won't see it?"

"I'll use my backpack. I carry it sometimes when I've got a big load."

I was hanging up when Aunt Queenie came in the back door. "Hi, Delrita. Any messages from Pop?"

"No messages for you," I said truthfully.

"Well, that's a relief. He had me running all over Jeff City this morning. First, he wanted chewing tobacco and the St. Louis paper. Then it was pajamas, which he can't wear with a cast on his leg. I declare. He's got me jumping through hoops."

"They could probably use you in the circus."

Aunt Queenie laughed. "I declare, Delrita. You've got your dad's droll sense of humor."

That laid a guilt trip on me. She wouldn't think I was funny if she knew about all this sneaking around behind her back.

Wednesday morning, I came within a hair of getting caught as I slipped out of Mr. Roebuck's room. Aunt Queenie's X-ray eyes missed the recorder in the backpack, but they saw right through me.

"Are you sick?" she asked, putting a hand on my forehead to check my temperature. I must have been cooler than I looked, because she let me out of the house.

I hoped Mr. Roebuck's stories were worth all the hassle. I was getting plenty of headaches out of the deal.

21

A Tough
Army Sergeant

"I can't believe it," I groaned as I stashed the backpack in my locker.

Avanelle peeked in at the tilting row of textbooks and the jacket on the hook. "What? Did you see a mouse or something?"

"Guess who forgot to bring her books."

"You didn't."

"Yes, I did. I'll have to call Aunt Queenie."

I elbowed my way down the hall to the pay phone outside the office. It ate two quarters before it rang my number.

"Hello?"

"Hi, Aunt Queenie. It's me."

"So you *are* sick. I knew you didn't look right when—"

"No, I'm fine. I forgot my books."

"Well, I declare, Delrita. Last week, it was gym clothes. Before that, your science report."

"I'm sorry. Would you—"

"No, I would not. I've got a meeting at city hall in fifteen minutes, and if I come by the school, I'll be late."

"But I could meet—"

"No, young lady, you'll just have to face the consequences. It's time you learned I wasn't put on this earth to serve at your beck and call. *You* are my responsibility, but seeing that you take your books to school is not."

My stomach lurched. She'd finally said it. I was her *responsibility*. Sophie Breech's poison dart was right on target.

"Delrita, are you there?"

"I'm here. Sorry I bothered you," I mumbled and hung up.

Maybe I am getting sick, I decided as I slunk into the office to buy a spiral notebook. My insides were churning—and my thoughts. Aunt Queenie hadn't volunteered for the job of raising me. I'd shown up on her doorstep. Been dumped in her lap.

The day was a disaster. I got scolded twice for not having my homework, I spilled glue in art class, and I slammed the locker door on my finger. In science class, someone knocked a jar off the shelf, splattering dead frogs and glass and formaldehyde all over the floor. The smell was nauseating.

When the last bell rang, I rushed out to the hall and gulped fresh air. It wasn't all that fresh—chalk dust, disinfectant, dirty sneakers, and sweat, and somebody somewhere had horse breath. The pushy, noisy mob of kids seemed worse this afternoon.

"Whew!" said Avanelle, stopping at my locker. "What's with the formaldehyde?"

"The cooks needed some for tomorrow's lunch."

She giggled. "Come on. I'm headed to Miss Myrtle's, so I'll walk with you for a couple of blocks."

Outside, when I didn't talk, she said, "I know you've had a rotten day, but I wish you weren't so quiet."

"I'm in great pain," I said, showing her the smashed and dented finger.

"Ouch."

I jostled the backpack. "And now I'm taking contraband to Mr. Roebuck. If he was a holy terror at the hospital, I hate to think what he'll be like at the nursing home."

"Just remember," she said solemnly, "the old guy's got emphysema and a broken leg. You can outrun him if you have to."

"Gee, thanks. You could have just wished me luck."

Ten minutes later, tape recorder in hand, I stood at the door to Orvis Roebuck's room. Two beds. One occupant. Had he already run off a roommate?

Since he didn't notice me right away, I stayed where I was and studied him. His left leg, in a cast, hung suspended from a traction device, and his bed was cranked up just enough for him to see the playing cards on his stomach. He was as drab as a black-and-white movie: gray face, gray hair, white cast, white hospital gown, white flabby biceps.

When he shifted position to move a card, two bits of color flashed on his forearms. The tattoos. The perfect rose on the left one, and the crudely lettered "Babe" on the right.

Again, I wondered if Babe had been a nickname for his wife. Saint Babe, the mother of Queen Esther. I smiled for the first time that day.

Mr. Roebuck spat in a Styrofoam cup, and barked, "Well, girlie, don't just stand there."

My smile faded as I inched into the room. "I'm delivering on my part of the deal."

"Come over and sit a spell. It's good to see somebody without a needle and a bedpan."

Cautiously, I laid the tape recorder on the bed, then perched on the edge of a chair facing him.

"Relax, girlie. I promise not to bite, if you'll tell me why you looked so happy to see me hanging here like a side of beef."

"I—I was just curious about your tattoos. They don't match. One's so neat, and the other one's—"

"Sloppy," finished Mr. Roebuck. "I never was very particular with my writin'."

"You did it?"

He cackled and showed me the "Babe" tattoo. "I was fifteen when I fell madly in love with a girl named Barb. Wrote her name myself with a sterilized needle wrapped in thread and dipped in ink. The romance didn't last much longer than the pain."

"Barb? But that says 'Babe.' "

"Years later, my little Rosie wanted me to change it, so I did." The old man's expression softened. "Rosie was my wife. Rose Ramona Roebuck. I used to tease her that her name sounded like revving up an engine." Tapping the rose tattoo, he said, "I had this one done for her in a tattoo parlor. Paid good money for it, and it's the one that gave me blood poisoning."

I winced. Vaccinations were bad enough. I'd never let somebody squirt ink under my skin.

Mr. Roebuck scooped up the cards and patted them into a stack. "Ain't it funny how life works out? I survived heavy artillery and machine-gun fire, and nearly went boots up over a danged old dirty needle."

I searched his face to see if he was teasing me. He wasn't.

"Rose decided it was her fault," he said. "Didn't matter to her that she was thousands of miles away when I had the tattoo done. She was a softhearted woman, the best I ever knew. Forty-six years we were married, and I never felt I was good enough for her. Six years ago, when she was all eat up with cancer, she wanted to leave the hospital and die at home. With help from the Good Lord, I was able to give her that. Course, Queen helped, too. She came every day to do the bathing, shampooing, things like that."

I was no longer perched on the chair like a bird ready to take off. This was a side of Orvis Roebuck I'd never seen— a tough army sergeant with doubts and feelings like everybody else, a man whose voice was gentle when he talked about his Rose.

I hadn't known that about Aunt Queenie, either. She'd talked about her mother, but not about the cancer, not about watching her die. No wonder she was preoccupied sometimes. Rose. Her mother's name was Rose. Was that why she was so attached to flowers?

The scar on Mr. Roebuck's cheek almost disappeared as

his wrinkles rearranged themselves in a frown. "I'm sorry, girlie. Don't know what's come over me, rattling on like this. It's like somebody pushed my talk button and I can't shut my mouth."

When he said "talk button," I remembered the tape recorder. That seemed like my cue to leave the room, but I didn't want to go.

"For a while after Rose died," Mr. Roebuck said, "I wanted to die, too. Then one day, I came across my duffel bag in the basement. Brought it upstairs and sorted through it. Saw my field kit, my boots and helmet and other combat gear. Made me realize just how short life is and how much I want to hang onto it." He stabbed a finger at the recorder. "Now this gizmo has got me to wondering all over again why a feller like me was spared in the war. A lot of good boys didn't make it."

At my questioning look, he said, "Some folks say that every man who showed up to fight was a hero, but I can't go along with that. I sure don't feel like no hero. My best friend—Leo—now there was a hero, and he ended up dead."

"Oh."

The room filled up with silence. Reluctantly, I stood up. "I—uh—guess I'd better go. The Marcums are expecting me."

"Be sure and come back before Queen shows up," said Mr. Roebuck. "Can't have her catching me with the gizmo. She'll get mad as fire 'cause I won't give her the tapes, and she'll fly off in a purple tizzy."

I managed to keep a straight face in front of him, but I had a good laugh as I walked down the hall. The queen in a purple tizzy. What an image that painted.

The sight of an empty wheelchair sobered me up and turned my thoughts around. I recalled how Aunt Queenie had converted the family room into a hospital room for Punky, how she'd cared for him so faithfully. I pictured her combing her mother's hair. Then I pictured Joey, walking a little taller as he wheeled his mother's chair.

A voice was rising and falling in the comatose woman's room. Passing by, I glanced inside, then stopped short and backed up. Unbelievable. Madeline Zang was sitting in a chair, reading poetry aloud.

No, this was a different woman. She had the same chestnut-colored hair as the lady on the bed, but she was as wrinkled as a Chinese shar-pei puppy. Head reared back, she was peering through silver-rimmed spectacles perched on the end of her nose.

I stood mesmerized as her voice tripped musically over the poem. Why put so much effort into reading to a person so out of touch? Why read to her at all?

Abruptly, the voice stopped, and the woman stared over the top of her glasses at me.

"Sorry," I mumbled, embarrassed to be caught gawking.

"Are you looking for someone?"

"No. I—uh. No."

"You're wondering why I'm reading to a person in this condition." It was a statement, not a question. She was probably used to curious stares.

I nodded.

"Because she's my daughter, and I want her to know that I'm here."

"She can—she can hear you?" I stammered.

"I don't know. If she can, the sound of my voice might bring her back. If she can't, it's a comfort to me that I've tried."

"Oh." Feeling awkward and intrusive, I moved out of her line of vision. I hoped she hadn't heard me laughing about the purple tizzy.

At the Marcums' room, I glanced inside. Mrs. Marcum was watching a talk show on TV. Joey, wearing his earphones, sat cross-legged on the bed, working on his sketch pad with a Magic Marker. The bandanna was tied around his neck.

"Knock, knock. I'm here."

Joey didn't look up. Maybe he didn't hear me because of the earphones. More likely, it was his way of saying, "Never disturb an artist at work."

"Come in," said Mrs. Marcum as she punched a button to mute the TV.

I walked in, my eyes on a sticklike woman on the screen. "Whoa. Look at that. She's almost as skinny as me."

But Mrs. Marcum had something weighty on her mind, and she didn't mince words. "So you want to take Joey to the circus."

Was she upset with Aunt Queenie for asking? Was she upset with me? I licked my lips. "Ye-es."

"Of course, I want my son to be happy, but all this talk

about equal opportunity for the handicapped . . . No, that's the wrong word. They don't call it 'handicapped' anymore."

"I know. It's 'people with disabilities.' "

"That's what I mean. Not 'disabled people,' but 'people with disabilities. Put the people first.' It sounds to me like a lot of fancy lingo that doesn't change anything. Plenty of folks still gawk and point and say rude things."

My hopes plummeted. I shouldn't have told her about those kids being afraid of Joey at the party.

"Your aunt talked a lot about your Punky, about spreading wings to fly. I think I'd like my Joey to be a little bird."

For a minute, it didn't sink in that she was saying yes. When it did, I hopped up and down. "Yay, Joey! You're going to the circus!"

His eyes stayed on the sketch pad.

I sat beside him on the bed, tore a sheet from my notebook, and said pointedly to his mother, "I'd create some magic, too, *if* I had some Magic Markers."

Without looking up, Joey removed the envelope full of markers from his pocket and plopped it on my lap.

I winked at Mrs. Marcum, who smiled and turned up the TV. While Joey colored his page blue, I made a rough sketch of Peanut and hid it in my pocket. If Joey saw it, he might want it, and I needed it for a pattern.

Soon he switched to a black marker and printed his name in big black letters: MRJOEYMARCUM.

"Mr. Joey Marcum," I said, "the next time I see you, we'll be on our way to Circus Vegas."

"Ya," he said, and gave me five.

• • •

"Thanks, girlie," said Mr. Roebuck as he handed over the tape recorder. "Telling those war stories, getting my feelings out where I can look at 'em, is a mighty big help in this place. Takes my mind off where I'm at."

"I'm glad."

He folded his arms and jerked his chin toward the hallway. "The old coot across the way snores like a bear in hibernation, and some old gal keeps walking up and down out there, hollering about an ironing board."

I bit back a smile. "Uh, Mr. Roebuck, can I ask you a question?"

"You can ask. I may not answer."

"Why did you glue the wing back on my swan?"

"You saw that, did you? Well, girlie, I've watched birds with broken wings. They flutter around, trying hard, but they can't get off the ground. They need somebody to care for them till they can fly away. Reckon I fixed your carving, 'cause sometimes when I look at you, I see a bird with a broken wing."

I almost dropped the tape recorder. That didn't sound like a man who resented having me in the house.

"You know, girlie, it's not good to keep things bottled up inside. I'm finding that out now with that recorder. Do you ever talk to Queen or Bert about your grief?"

"Not much," I said, letting my gaze fall to the tan bedspread. "Aunt Queenie's so busy with her . . . *responsibilities*. And Uncle Bert's a brother to my mom and Punky. How could I talk to him about their dying?"

"That's what I thought. I knew, soon as I moved into

that house, there were too many things left unsaid. Tell you what, girlie, I know a little about grief myself. If you ever want to talk, I've got two ears."

I studied him. His face was kind, his blue eyes sad. Had I misinterpreted the sour expressions, the piercing stares? Had I been seeing only what I wanted to see—a grouchy old man?

"Girlie," he said, "you recollect what I told you about that turtle on the fence post?"

I nodded, but I couldn't make the connection. What did the turtle have to do with me keeping things bottled up?

"That old turtle couldn't get off of that fence post without help. Somebody had to run interference. I'm offering to do the same for you. If you need to talk, I'm willing to listen. Can't have you carrying the weight of your grief all by yourself."

"Thanks, Mr. Roebuck. I'll remember that." I started to leave, but something held me back. At last, I said in a small voice, "Mr. Roebuck, I've been wrong about you."

"Wrong? Whadda you mean?"

"I thought you didn't like having me in the house."

He pulled on his lower lip and gave that some thought. "Reckon I can see why you'd feel that way. I've been real contrary since I moved in with Queen. She's my daughter and I love her, but she's the world's best at lighting my fuse. It was good that she pampered her mother, but I don't want her pampering me. I'm not helpless. Wasn't, anyway, until I broke my danged leg."

"At least, it's temporary."

"Now don't you be trying to sweeten my disposition. I

figure if I'm crotchety enough, Queen'll pitch one of her purple tizzies."

"You *want* her to get mad?"

"Yup," he said, his eyes crinkling with mischief. "I'll tell her to take her complaints to the advisory board. Maybe they'll kick me out."

22

The War

We were eating baked chicken and rice when Aunt Queenie said, "The advisory board has called an emergency meeting for tonight."

Two thoughts collided in my brain. One, the meeting probably meant trouble for Avanelle's dad. Two, I'd be home free with Mr. Roebuck's tapes, because Uncle Bert had a deacons' meeting at church.

Aunt Queenie clicked her nails on the table. "Somehow it leaked out that Trezane was questioned about those burglaries. I don't understand it. Since Trezane wasn't charged, that information should have remained confidential."

I made swirls in my rice with my fork. Telephone, telegraph, tell-a-Tree.

"I expect your meeting'll last half the night," Uncle Bert said. "Mine should be over by nine."

"Well, I declare, Delrita," Aunt Queenie said, her painted-on eyebrows knitting together in a frown. "We're leaving you alone so much lately. I feel as though we're shirking our responsibility."

Responsibility.

I remembered how carefree Aunt Queenie had been after visiting her father in the hospital. I could still see her breezing in the door, singing "I'm home," and carrying that bag of fried chinny.

"Delrita," she said, "is something wrong with your dinner?"

"No. Why?"

"You've been chasing that bite with your fork for five minutes. I declare. Here you are, picking at your food in the land of plenty, while the church sends supplies to people starving in Bangladesh."

Face it, Delrita, I told myself. You're a disappointment. A misfit. A project that isn't working out.

I tried to swallow back the hurt, but it wouldn't go away.

As soon as I was alone in the house, I zipped to my room, so I could carve and listen to Mr. Roebuck's tapes. After setting up the recorder, I laid out items from my Barbie case.

My crude Magic Marker sketch of Joey's bear reminded me of the woodcarving term *happy mistake.* That's an accidental cut in the basswood that doesn't ruin the carving, but adds a surprising dimension to the piece.

Today, I'd discovered a surprising dimension to Mr. Roebuck. Rough on the outside, but a happy mistake underneath. Thinking of that made me feel better. Made me forget for a while that I was a big disappointment to Aunt Queenie.

I sat down, picked up my knife, and punched PLAY. First came some buzzing and mumbling, and then the gravelly voice:

"This is retired Master Sergeant Orvis Roebuck, U.S. Army Infantry, recording memories of World War Two. Hmmmpfff. 'Memories' makes it sound like a picnic or a night on the town, something pleasant you'd want to remember, but it sure as ———— wasn't pleasant at all."

I smiled at that little skip on the tape, where Mr. Roebuck had cleaned up some pollution.

"I've never talked about the war before, but I reckon there's a first time for everything. Might as well start at the beginning and tell why I joined up. It was Leo Garrison's fault. Leo and me grew up on neighboring farms, and when we weren't helping our dads in the fields, we were exploring caves, fishing, skinny-dipping. Halloweens, we tipped over the neighbors' outhouses, and once we had to run like the devil when Elvin Moon caught us painting his cow green. We kept working the farms after we finished school, 'cause that's all we really knew.

"And then the United States entered World War Two. Folks everywhere gathered around the radio at night, listening to the news. Leo took it personal when it sounded like the Allies were losing ground. He kept threatening to sign up, although as a farmer, he wouldn't have had to go. One day, he went to town and enlisted. Since I couldn't talk him out of it, I enlisted, too. Couldn't let him leave me in Missouri, staring at the rear end of a blamed old mule. . . ."

Mr. Roebuck talked about being trained as a heavy machine gunner, getting separated from Leo, letters from Rose, and censored mail. I was finishing the bear's snout when the tape stopped.

I turned it over and hit PLAY again. Soon Mr. Roebuck's voice took on a different tone. I stared at the recorder. He sounded breathless and excited. No, he sounded scared.

I sat spellbound, listening. The hair raised on my arms. That voice was transporting me from Tangle Nook, Missouri, to just off the coast of England at the dawn of D-Day, June sixth, nineteen forty-four.

"We were aboard a ship, waiting for orders to cross the English Channel into Normandy. The sky was black with Allied planes taking off into the fog and wind and cold. Thousands of planes—fighters and C-47s—and their roar was like the wrath of God.

"For hours, we stood on that deck and watched pure conflagration. Our planes were bombing, and our ships were shelling, and we knew the first wave of infantry was heading for the beaches. I was shaking in my boots and torn in three directions. Knowing I had to get in there and do my part to end the blasted war. Itching to whip Leo for getting me into such a mess. Wishing I was home and staring at that old mule's behind.

"Next day, June seventh, I found out my fear was justified. That first wave of troops had been lambs sent to slaughter. Big German guns blasted at their landing crafts, filling the sea with bodies. The survivors waded ashore in water red with blood.

"When our company's orders came at noon, we waded

in with our guns held over our heads. Utah Beach it was. Still slippery with blood.

"By then, the Allies had tanks and bulldozers on the beach, but the Nazis were just beyond. For days and days, we fought our way inland, with never a break from the planes strafing overhead and the shrapnel falling. But the biggest danger was enemy snipers, hiding in an awful maze of hedgerows.

"One day, I was hiding in a hedgerow myself on the outskirts of a village. Had my gun trained on a house where we'd seen some Nazi activity, when I sensed that I was being watched. As I jerked around, a sniper's bullet ripped through my face. Knocked me out cold. When I came to, I was on a bed in an old house, and an American rifleman was standing guard at a window. When we heard shooting outside, he moved me and the mattress to the floor, and I blacked out again. Next time I came to, the American was gone, and three Nazi soldiers were firing machine guns out the windows.

"I was hoping the Nazis would shoot me, to stop the pain in my face. My right jaw was fractured, my top teeth on the left had been blown to bits, and the hole in my cheek burned like ————. I was lying on something sticky. I felt around. Felt blood. Felt another man's body. The rifleman. I was nearly out of my head with pain, so I don't know if the blood was mine or his. All I know is, he was dead. There was blood on the mattress, on the floor, on the walls, on his body. So much blood. For three days, they kept me on the mattress with the dead man. No food. No water. . . ."

Lights from a car outside flashed at the edge of my window shade. I lifted the shade and saw Uncle Bert's Lincoln pulling into the drive.

"Crud," I said aloud. In the last few minutes, Mr. Roebuck's story had become more to me than a history assignment. I was itching to play the rest of the tape, but it was too risky now. I hid the recorder and got ready for bed.

Every time I closed my eyes, I saw a bloody mattress. I gave up trying to sleep, hauled out the bear, and whittled its bandanna.

At eleven forty-five, I was crawling back under the covers when Aunt Queenie came home. I jumped up and met her in the hall. "How'd it go?"

With a sigh, she slumped against the wall and slipped off her shoes. "We voted to keep Trezane Shackleford on the job, but on probation for thirty days."

"Good deal."

"Yes, it is. I'm just too tired to appreciate it at the moment."

Her crow's feet were prominent, and her topknot was drooping to one side. Sophie Breech would be happy to know she was showing her age. "Aunt Queenie?"

"Yes."

"You look beat. Why don't you sleep late in the morning?"

"Well, I declare, Delrita. I couldn't do that. Seeing you off to school is my responsibility."

There it was again. Responsibility. Now that I knew the truth, that word was worse than a sore thumb for getting in the way.

· · ·

I'd never before played hooky from school, but I was tempted to do it Thursday morning so I could listen to Mr. Roebuck's tapes. No. What I really wanted was to sit with him and hear everything he knew about the war. When Aunt Queenie got a call asking her to work someone else's shift at the crisis center, I settled for visiting her father after school.

At three-thirty on the dot, I was standing in his doorway, my eyes on the scar where the sniper's bullet had ripped through his face.

"Well, hello, girlie! I wasn't expecting you back so soon."

I marched in and set the recorder beside him on the bed. "Aunt Queenie's filling in at the crisis center. We're safe till five o'clock."

He gave me that lopsided grin. "Did you get anywhere on your report?"

"Writing, no. Listening, yes. I got up to the part where you—uh—found the body of the rifleman."

The grin turned upside down. Mr. Roebuck fingered the scar and stared at the wall with watery eyes. I figured he was seeing a bloody mattress.

"I'm sorry," I murmured.

"War is horrible," he said to the wall. "Good men die. Brave men. Men like that rifleman and my friend Leo." He wiped his forehead with a red handkerchief, then let it slide across his eyes.

I drew a deep breath and ventured, "Mr. Roebuck, yesterday you told me if I'm willing to talk, you're willing to listen. Does that road run both ways? Are you willing to talk and let *me* listen?"

"What're you gettin' at, girlie?"

"Tell me what happened after you got shot. I want to hear the story now, not wait till it's safe to play the tapes. I want it straight from the horse's mouth."

His eyes bored into mine. I didn't dare blink. Or breathe.

"Why?" he asked.

"Because I've been thinking about it since last night, and I've got to know. It's—it's the first time I ever saw the human side of war."

He mopped his forehead again. He coughed. "All right, girlie. I'll tell you the rest of it, face to face. Tape what I say if you need to, but don't distract me by taking notes. And one more thing. When you write about me, get it straight."

I nodded and reached for the tape recorder, but I had no doubt I'd get it straight. The bullet in the face, the bloody mattress, the dead rifleman were stamped on my brain in indelible ink.

I fast-forwarded the tape to a blank spot, then stood still, waiting for Mr. Roebuck to gather his thoughts. His eyes were distant now, his hands twisting and untwisting the handkerchief.

At last, he motioned that he was ready. I punched the right button on the recorder and eased myself into a chair.

"I was so weak from pain and blood loss and lack of water," he began, "I just lay there waiting—and hoping—to die. On the fourth day, a Nazi officer came to the house, babbling '*Befragen, befragen.*' Interrogate. I'll never forget his shiny jackboots stomping toward me, crunching through broken glass. I thought I was a goner then, and it came to me that I wanted to live. The officer tried to question me, but he couldn't speak very good English and I couldn't say much but gibberish. He finally just kicked me in the ribs and barked some orders at the soldiers.

"They hauled me off to some sorry excuse for a hospital. Dirty. No antibiotics. No medicine at all, except some bluish ointment. Hair fell out from high fever. Infection raised big blisters on my body that broke and then swelled up again.

"The prisoners' food was moldy black bread and broth. I couldn't eat the bread, 'cause it made me bleed to chew. The broth was nasty—real nasty. Probably made from dog or cat or horse meat. What was worse, we could smell the food the Nazis ate—chicken and eggs and fresh vegetables. They must have plundered every farm in the countryside.

"The fighting was never far away. Heard big guns going off every night, and in the mornings, the air was full of smoke. I was slowly starving to death and too weak to lift my head, so when Leo showed up, I thought I was hallucinating. I didn't even know he was in that half of the world, but there he was with his left leg all shot up. When he saw the shape I was in, he vowed that somehow he'd help me. Course, I figured he was just in shock and talking crazy. He was a prisoner, too, with only one good leg. How could he help me?"

I couldn't take my eyes off Mr. Roebuck. I was a prisoner myself, captivated by his story. My chest felt tight from shallow breathing.

"Turned out, Leo was a miracle God sent to me. He came up with a pair of crutches, and he found another patient who knew a little something about dentistry. That fellow wired my jaws shut so I wouldn't keep breaking open the hole in my face.

"The next morning, Leo showed up with two raw eggs and poured the slimy things down my throat. This went on for a couple more days, and when I had to strength to do it, I asked him about those eggs.

"Seems some of the guards were pretty lax, 'cause they didn't expect a bunch of half-dead men to cause them any trouble. Leo'd been slipping into the kitchen at night and helping himself to eggs. 'No more,' I said. 'Too dangerous.' But he wouldn't stop. 'Gotta do it,' he said. 'You'd do the same . . . for me.' "

Mr. Roebuck's voice cracked on the last two words. The cords in his neck were quivering, and he was wheezing violently. I inched closer to the call button at the head of the bed, in case I had to ring for a nurse.

For a while, he couldn't speak. The tape recorder whirred softly, a counterpoint to the wheezing.

Finally, he rasped, "For almost two weeks, I lived on raw eggs, and then one morning, Leo was gone. Just disappeared. I waited and waited, and prayed more than I've ever prayed in my life, but I knew in my heart the guards had shot him."

Tears ran in rivulets down Mr. Roebuck's cheeks. He wiped them away with the back of his hand.

I felt tears on my own cheeks, felt my nose running. I needed a tissue from that box on the nightstand, but I was afraid to move. If I broke the spell, he might send me away so he could cry in private.

Mr. Roebuck was staring at the handkerchief as if he'd never seen it before. Then he came to himself and blew his nose. "Sorry, girlie," he said. "I'll get through this if it's the last thing I do."

I reached for a tissue and blew my nose, too.

"Two days later, the Allies liberated the village. When they carried me out on a stretcher, I was stinking and filthy. They flew me to a hospital in England. Patched me up and sent me back to the States, and that's where I was when the war ended. For Leo, the war ended back in that little village. I was helpless and dying, and he saved my life. I was the turtle he set off the post. To this day, I haven't figured out why Leo was the one who had to die. He was a hero, a much better man than me."

Chest heaving, Mr. Roebuck turned his face into his pillow and closed his eyes. "So there you are, girlie," he said weakly. "I'm done. Take that gizmo when you leave and don't bring it no more. I've said all I'm gonna say about the dad-blamed war."

I shut off the tape recorder. I wanted to comfort Mr. Roebuck, but I knew instinctively this was not the time. Nothing I could say would ease the pain he was feeling now.

I sat by his bed until his breathing leveled out, and soon the rhythmic movement of his chest told me he was sleeping. Carrying the tape recorder, I tiptoed to the door—and cringed at the squeak when I opened it.

"Hold it right there, girlie!"

I spun around. "Yes, sir?"

"You've got your war story. Does that mean you won't be coming back?"

"I—uh—do you want me to?"

"You bet I do. You don't need a walker, you're not shriveled as a prune, and you haven't lost your ironing board."

"Now there's a compliment if I ever heard one," I said. Then I snapped a salute and quoted General Douglas MacArthur: " 'I shall return.' "

23

The Hero Speech

The house was deserted when I got home. After depositing my backpack and books on the kitchen table, I took the tape recorder into Mr. Roebuck's room and closed the door. A shaft of late-afternoon sunlight cut across the black-and-tan spread.

The room was different now, and not just because Aunt Queenie had vacuumed the tobacco specks and cellophane from the carpet and stacked the newspapers and magazines into a pile. The difference was in me, in my opinion of her father.

I thought of the sniper's bullet ripping through his face. His will to live when he saw those Nazi jackboots crunching through broken glass. The bleeding when he tried to chew. The raw eggs sliding down his throat. . . . Mrs. Bagby was right. Many moving stories of war have never been printed in the history books.

I walked over and studied the triangle-shaped arrangement of photos and certificates on the wall. On the top row were three eight-by-tens in black and white: Half a dozen young men in fatigues gathered around a Jeep. A soldier cleaning his rifle. That same soldier with his arm slung loosely over Orvis Roebuck's shoulders. Under the glass in this photo was a button stamped "U.S. Army."

On the second row hung the certificates and medals for the Bronze Star and the Purple Heart. A lump came to my throat. Before today, war had been something that didn't have much to do with me. Now I ached for Mr. Roebuck, who'd fought the battles and felt the fear and been scarred by memories and a sniper's bullet.

Below the medals was a color photograph of Master Sergeant Roebuck in full army dress. His solemn expression was fitting, because his backdrop was the American flag he'd fought to defend.

I turned around. My swan was still on the dresser, caught now in a beam of sunlight. Thanks to Mr.—no, *Sergeant* Roebuck, my pretty bird, once broken, was all mended and ready to soar. I smiled. I'd once seen the swan as wasted hours, wasted work. Now I saw it as a happy mistake.

Slowly, I walked to the closet, my eyes on Uncle Sam. He was guarding the duffel bag, his stern glance saying, "Don't touch it."

The closet smelled the same—of cedar and dust and old metal. When I saw the lumpy canvas bag slumped against the wall, I thought of a dead man on a bloody mattress. I wasted no time pulling the bag's drawstring and shoving the recorder in beside the helmets. I whipped the door shut and leaned against it, but jumped away when I remembered Uncle Sam.

I slept hard and woke up early—in time to hear "The Star-Spangled Banner" on the radio.

Up, dummy.

I hauled myself out of bed, my mind on Sergeant Roebuck. He didn't think he was a hero, but I certainly did—and I intended to tell him so after school. I even rehearsed a hero speech in the shower.

By six-fifteen, I was all dressed up with no place to go. It was too early to eat breakfast and too early to walk to Avanelle's. The time was right to finish carving Joey's bear.

With an awl, I etched lines to represent stitching on the fabric of the paws, and I made tiny holes beside the mouth to represent whiskers. With a spoon gouge, I deepened the grooves under the arms, and I took a sliver off one ear. At last, the carving was as good as I could make it. The bear looked up at me with its one pale wooden eye, and I felt a little glow of pride.

Sergeant Roebuck, his face puckered in concentration, was scratching inside his cast with the hook of a coat hanger. When he saw me in the doorway, he stopped scratching and grinned. "Hello, girlie. Come on in."

I suddenly felt all flustered and tongue-tied, unable to remember the speech I'd been practicing off and on all day. "I—uh—don't want to bother you."

"No bother. Come in and take a load off."

Sitting down didn't help my thinker. I fidgeted in the chair.

"What's wrong, girlie? Is it Queen? Did she find the gizmo?"

"No. That's not it."

"Then what's wrong? What's on your mind?"

"You. And the war."

Sergeant Roebuck frowned. "It was all that blubbering I did yesterday. Sorry, girlie. Remembering got to me."

"It wasn't the blubbering. I did some of that myself."

"Well, then, what is it you came to say?"

"That you were—uh—brave. You enlisted, the same as Leo, when you could have stayed on the farm, staring at the rear end of a blamed old mule."

Some hero speech. Whoopee.

"Girlie, I was scared out of my mind from the time I boarded that ship in the English Channel until they flew me out of France."

"Who wouldn't be? Wherever Leo did his fighting, I'll bet he was scared, too."

"I wouldn't know," said the sergeant as he picked lint off the bedspread. "Didn't see him until we were both shot up and stuck in that filthy hospital. I was in no shape to ask, and he never said."

"But he was a human being. Didn't he run like the devil the night you boys painted that cow green?"

Sergeant Roebuck shot me a look of surprise.

"I didn't mean that as an insult to Leo," I said hastily. "I just meant that after he saved your life, he might have gotten bigger in your eyes."

"I know, girlie, and it's strange. You and I seem to be of the same mind. Since yesterday, I've been looking at things from a different perspective. Doing a little soul-searching, too. I told you Leo was sneaking those eggs out of the kitchen. The truth is, he was stealing those eggs from the Nazis. He was stealing to save my life, but he was stealing just the same. It gave me pause, to borrow a phrase from Queen. Made me think I've been a little rough on that Shackleford fellow. Maybe he was stealing 'cause his kids were hungry."

"He didn't steal at all. He thought he was helping some guys move furniture. And if the police still consider him a suspect in those robberies, they're barking up the wrong tree."

One corner of Sergeant Roebuck's mouth turned up, and then the other, until he was wearing his regular lopsided smile. "Sounds to me like you're sold on the man. Or maybe it's the boy, Tree?"

"Both," I admitted as heat rushed to my cheeks.

If Sergeant Roebuck noticed my discomfort, he didn't let on. "Well," he said, "as of today, I'm turning over a new leaf. It's time for me to stop passing out the judgment and lend a hand—help the turtle off the fence post, so to speak. I've even thought of a way to do it."

"How?"

"By letting your Mr. Shackleford use my wheels while I'm laid up."

I caught my breath. "Your little red truck?"

"It's the only truck I've got." He looked away from me,

as if embarrassed himself now. Focusing on the cast, he poked the hanger inside it and scratched his leg again.

"Sergeant Roebuck?"

His chin came up at my use of his title. "Yes, girlie?"

"It's none of my business, but I think you should stop passing judgment on yourself."

"On myself?"

"Yes. Haven't you been doing that since your wife . . . since you took that duffel bag out of the basement? You said it reminded you how short life is, but I think you've been using it to torture yourself with the past. Why do you need combat gear? So you can feel guilty about Leo every time you see it? *You* didn't kill him. The Nazis did. Maybe you need to think about that."

"That gear is important to me. The helmets . . ." Sergeant Roebuck's voice trailed off, and his eyes glazed. "My helmet saved me from a bullet once, before the sniper. The other one's . . . Leo's."

I leaned forward in my chair, anxious to hear more.

"After he disappeared from the hospital, somebody brought me his helmet, his little black Bible, and a button he'd lost off his uniform. My rescuers thought I was loco, 'cause when they hauled me out of that hospital and put me on the plane, I wouldn't let go of Leo's belongings. Way I felt about it, I couldn't bring his body out of Normandy, but I could bring that little part of him back to the States. I sent the Bible to his folks. The button's with his photo, under glass. If Queen wasn't so danged particular, his helmet would be on the dresser, 'stead of in the closet."

"Maybe it's just as well," I said. "In my room, I've got a picture of my parents and one little keepsake—a God's eye. The rest of their stuff is boxed up, out of sight, because it would hurt too much to look at it every day."

Sergeant Roebuck folded his hands and twiddled his thumbs—forward, backward, forward again. "Out of the mouths of babes," he grunted.

"What?"

"You're awful young, girlie, but you've taught this old man a good lesson: Keep a few memories out in the open and store the rest away."

24

The Circus

That evening, it took me forever to get ready for the circus. I tried on half the clothes in my closet, in search of an outfit that would knock Tree's eyes out. I settled on a long-sleeved, hunter green shirt with socks to match, black loafers, and black jeans. I brushed my hair and put on blush, lipstick, and a hint of green eye shadow. After studying the overall effect in the mirror, I added gold barrettes to my hair—the idea being that if all else failed, Tree would be dazzled by reflected light.

When I'd done all I could do, I went looking for Aunt Queenie. She was in the family room, crocheting a mile a minute and listening to Uncle Bert read a piece from the newspaper.

What a contrast they were in the lamplight. He was rumpled and shiny, while she was fresh and powdered. Her pantsuit, the pencil in her topknot, and her newly manicured nails were all the same shade of lavender.

My eagle eyes focused on the yarn on her hook. Green. Uh-oh. She'd started cranking out doodads for my room.

"You're ready," said Aunt Queenie. "So am I." She stashed the crochet in her tote bag, then stood up with the bag on her arm.

"You're not taking that to the circus," I said.

"I certainly am. It'll give me something to do."

"You don't need something to do. You'll be watching the show."

"I don't want to watch. I want to crochet."

"Aunt Queenie, if you make doodads at the circus, I'll die of embarrassment."

"Doodads? Well, I declare."

"Delrita has a point," said Uncle Bert. "Maybe you should leave that stuff here."

"Maybe I should have my head examined for agreeing to do this in the first place," she sniffed, tossing the bag on her chair.

At the nursing home, Aunt Queenie waited in the car while I went in to pick up Joey.

His room reeked of spicy cologne, and his bed held a tangle of clothing turned inside out. Like me, Joey had gone overboard getting ready for the circus.

Clad in a pale blue western shirt and jeans, his curls brushed to a golden sheen, he was stooped before his mother, who was tying the bandanna around his neck. It was awkward for both of them. While he wobbled in that unnatural position, she struggled to tie a knot with her clawlike hands.

"Need some help?" I asked from the doorway.

"M-m-my mama," replied Joey with a shake of his head.

"Hi, Delrita." Mrs. Marcum smiled, finished tying the knot, and patted Joey's cheek. "There you go, son."

"Ya." He came hotfooting across the room, yanked on his cowboy boots, snatched up Peanut, and hurried back to kiss his mom. I barely had time to say "good-bye" before he was hustling me down the hall.

Outside, he hopped into the front seat, and as I was fastening his safety belt, he checked out Aunt Queenie's feet.

"No red shoes this time," she said.

Sticking his short legs straight out, he grinned and waggled Peanut at his boots.

At the Shacklefords', Birdie cried, "Hey, red ones!" at sight of Joey's boots. She scampered over him and sat so close, Randolph had to crawl over them both.

Avanelle, Eddie, and Tree climbed into the back with me.

Tree leaned forward and sized me up when we were underway. "Velveeta," he said, "the weather is *awesome.*"

A coded compliment for his all-weather friend! My heart felt zapped by lightning.

Avanelle nudged me in the ribs. I expected a wisecrack about Tree, but she said, "Isn't this exciting? I've never seen a circus, and I've never been inside the Regency."

"It's a theater in the round," said Aunt Queenie. "Magnificent. They lay false panels to protect the floor. Still, it gives me pause that equipment and animals will—"

"Yay! Animals!" yelled Birdie. "There'll be lions and tigers and elephants and . . . Uh-oh. Where they gonna poop?"

"Well, I declare," said Aunt Queenie.

"Birdie, that's embarrassing," said Avanelle.

"Well, I just wanna know."

Tree winked at me, and my heart zapped again. At this rate, I'd need CPR before the night was over.

At the Regency, we presented our tickets, then passed through double doors and stood gawking. We weren't in an auditorium. We were under the big top of a three-ring circus, complete with sawdust on the floor. Stanchions, nets, tightropes. Five tigers circling in a cage. A dozen workers in jeans and red CIRCUS VEGAS T-shirts.

Tree led the way to seats on the sixth row of the bleachers, and we filled them up like falling dominoes. He sat first, followed by Eddie, Joey, me, Birdie, Avanelle, Randolph, and Aunt Queenie.

Organ music blared. More people poured in, and vendors roamed the bleachers with their wares. When Aunt Queenie bought popcorn and Sno-Cones for all of us, I offered to hold Peanut for Joey, but he shook his head and planted the bear between his knees.

Soon the organ played a buildup, and a spotlight pinpointed a man in a scarlet uniform, a black top hat, and tall black boots. In a booming voice, he told us he was Rufus Rainwater, our ringmaster, and he welcomed us to Circus Vegas.

"For your first thrill of the night," he said, sweeping his arm to the right, "I present the ravishing Miss Felina, tamer of the big cats!"

All eyes turned to the tiger cage, where a lady in a skimpy costume of pink sequins and black lace stood shimmering under the lights. The tigers, tails switching, sat perched on stools in front of her like obedient pets.

"The biggest cat is King Tut," said Rufus Rainwater. "He's a Bengal tiger ten feet long, weighing five hundred fourteen pounds. Miss Felina, show us what King Tut can do."

The tamer cracked her whip, and King Tut sprang to the ground and circled the cage on his hind legs.

One by one, the other cats did the same.

"Don't be fooled by the seeming docility of these creatures," said the ringmaster. "They're wild animals, and none have been declawed. If one of them were to attack Miss Felina, we couldn't do much beyond spraying it with a fire extinguisher. Tranquilizer bullets don't work fast enough, and real bullets would endanger this crowd of people."

A hush fell over the audience, broken only by King Tut, who let out a bloodcurdling roar.

I glanced quickly left, then right. The Shacklefords were all freckles and eyeballs. Joey, too, sat as if hypnotized. Only Aunt Queenie looked bored.

The tigers showed their stuff—balancing balls, limboing under a pole, jumping through a hoop, and finally, jumping through a ring of fire.

The crowd was still applauding when the spotlight angled toward the ceiling. "And now, ladies and gentlemen," said Rufus Rainwater, "cast your eyes overhead at the fabulous Favio on the flying trapeze. . . ."

After Favio came five acrobat clowns, tooling around the arena in a tiny car. On their second round, they chased three other clowns who backflipped to get out of their way. Soon all eight clowns were on the ground, squirting each other with bottled seltzer water. Through it all, Tree howled with laughter, and Joey jiggled with glee.

Next came a sword swallower, a juggler, a magician, more clowns, and three dancing elephants.

As the elephants were lumbering toward the exit, Birdie laid her head in Avanelle's lap and yawned. "If I go to sleep," she said, "will somebody clap my hands for me?"

She missed the stunt riders on horseback and the human pyramid. Rufus Rainwater was announcing the grand finale—a tightrope walker performing without a safety net—when I realized Joey was jiggling double-time. One glance told me this wasn't glee, but an emergency.

"Do you need a restroom?" I asked.

"Ya." Instantly, he was up and barreling between people on the bleachers.

I looked to Tree, but Eddie was asleep in his arms. No time to waste. I'd lose Joey once he reached those double doors. "We'll meet you in the lobby," I told Avanelle and streaked off in Joey's wake.

When we reached the hallway where the restrooms were, he had to run all the way.

The restroom had no door—only a wall inside to block the view. I stayed on alert in the hallway, listening for any noise that might mean someone was bothering Joey. Silence. I glanced back at the lobby, making sure a security guard was within hollering distance.

Coming toward me was a clown wearing an orange wig, a painted frown, and a suit with giant polka dots. He nodded at me before entering the restroom. I smiled and stood listening for Joey's reaction when he saw the clown, close up.

"Ya!" The word bounced off the concrete walls.

I heard snatches of conversation, a clank, squirts, and giggles. What was going on?

Another clank. More squirts. More giggles. Just when I thought I should yell for the guard, Joey emerged from the restroom, his shirt front splattered and his Elvis buckle dripping water.

"Joey! I was worried! How come you're so wet?"

He held up a seltzer bottle.

"He spotted that in my pocket," said the clown, coming up behind him, "and I let him squirt the sinks. The bottle is his to keep."

"Thanks—I think."

The hall was filling up with people. Joey showed his seltzer bottle to a huge man with an earring, a girl in a circus T-shirt, and a woman with two kids. I kept my eyes glued to his stubby fingers, for fear he'd give someone a squirt.

It was going on eleven o'clock, and we were stuck in the snarl of traffic leaving the Regency. Up front, between Aunt Queenie and Joey, Randolph wiggled and talked nonstop about the circus, while Birdie groused that he was hogging the seat.

"M-m-my mama," said Joey for the umpteenth time.

"Soon, Joey," sighed Aunt Queenie, the lights from the

dashboard outlining her tight jaw. She inched us forward another foot or so, then sat clicking her fingernails on the steering wheel.

"M-m-my mama," Joey said again.

"Randolph's touching me," whined Birdie.

". . . be a juggler, too," said Randolph.

Avanelle reached over the seat and clamped a hand on his head to stop his squirming. "Randolph, give it a rest. Wait and tell Mom and Dad when we get home."

"Well, sis," Tree said, "at least we know he enjoyed the circus. So did I. It was great."

"Did you pick up any pointers from the clowns?" I asked, and grinned at the thought of pointing Heidi Grissom back to Arkansas.

"I'm gonna buy a seltzer bottle."

Avanelle snorted. "Don't even *think* about squirting me."

"M-m-my mama."

"Joey," said Aunt Queenie, "I promise to take you home first. In fact, if we're not out of here in five minutes, I'll park this car and *walk* you to your mama."

"M-m-my mama."

A few minutes later, the traffic cleared. We sailed across town to the nursing home, and Joey and I bailed out.

" 'Bye, Joey," said the Shackleford kids.

"Ya." He took my hand and hurried me inside.

The lights were dim, the building creepy quiet, except for the burbling of the aquarium. A woman at the nurses' station frowned when she saw us approaching. Was she unhappy because Joey had a seltzer bottle? Because I'd kept him out so late? Because the excitement of the circus might have put a strain on his heart?

The woman's face stayed puckered, like someone eating a green persimmon. She jumped up and intercepted me with the words, "I'll take over from here."

Relinquishing Joey's hand to her, I said, " 'Bye, Joey. I'm glad you got to see the circus."

"Ya."

I watched them walk away. Watched Joey's familiar shuffle. Something didn't feel right, but I couldn't figure out what it was. Then it hit me like a brick. Joey didn't have Peanut.

"Peanut!" he said suddenly, stopping in his tracks.

Persimmon tried to pull him along. "Come on, hon. It's late."

Joey wouldn't budge.

"You're always misplacing that bear," she said. "We'll find him in the morning."

"Peanut."

"In the *morning,* Joey. It's late."

Joey burst into tears. Persimmon dug a tissue from her pocket and wiped his nose and mouth. "Sssssh. Quiet. The boss'll have my head if you wake everybody up."

He let out a keening sound that echoed down the hall.

Persimmon glared at me, spurring me to action. I signaled to her that I would check the car. I raced outside, then raced back in, dejected, without the bear.

There was Joey at the nurse's station, listening on the phone.

"Nine-one-one?" I asked Persimmon.

She nodded. "The paramedics talk to him. Calm him down."

But talking wouldn't solve the problem this time. Peanut wasn't just misplaced. He was *lost* somewhere between here and the circus.

"Ya." That was Joey signing off.

"Joey," I said as he replaced the receiver, "I'll search high and low until I find him."

"Ya." His bad eye was mostly white, but his good eye gleamed with hope.

I felt a quivering in my knees. What if I'd just promised him the moon?

"We'll check lost-and-found first thing in the morning," said Aunt Queenie, easing her arm out from under the sleeping Birdie.

"We can't wait that long," I argued. "Peanut might get swept up in the trash, and we'd never find him."

"But it's after eleven. And look, these little ones are worn out."

"Please, Aunt Queenie. Can't we drop them off and go *now?* Joey loves Peanut." Desperately, I added, "Think how Punky would have felt if he'd lost his cowboy hat."

She whirled around to look at me. Her face was in shadow, but I knew I'd struck a nerve. She'd personally seen to it that Punky was buried with his cowboy hat—back when Uncle Bert and I were too numb with grief to think. "Well, I declare, Delrita," she huffed as she slipped the car into drive. "You certainly know which buttons to press to get what you want. I'll have to call Bert from the Regency, or he'll think we've been knocked on the head and hijacked."

I let my breath escape and leaned back in the seat.

When we reached the Shacklefords', Tree stayed in the car. "If it's all the same to you," he said, "I want to help find Peanut."

A security guard stopped us in the lobby. When I told him why we'd come, he said, "Go ahead, but you're probably too late. Those cleanup crews work fast."

While Aunt Queenie hurried to a pay phone and Tree ran down to check the men's room, I rushed into the auditorium—and stood gawking as I had before the circus.

Gone was the illusion of a big top. The bleachers had been folded back, the areas under them swept clean. A small army of workers in red T-shirts and jeans was dismantling the circus equipment. A janitor in a gray uniform was driving a Bobcat loader and scooping up sawdust. Another janitor was pushing a broom, and two more were hoisting planks off the floor.

I spoke to the man with the broom. "Did you find a bear?"

He stopped sweeping and drawled, "Weren't no bear in this circus, hon. Just tigers and eleph—"

"No, I mean a teddy bear. Brown and furry. Red neckerchief. One eye missing. He might have fallen through the bleachers."

"Then we prob'ly swept him up." He asked his coworkers, but they were no help at all. "Sorry, hon," he said.

"When you're wading through a ton of trash, you don't pay much attention to what's there. You can check for yourself if you want. Barrels are in the basement. We'll be compacting the stuff when we finish here. Don't get your hopes up, though. Lotsa kids here tonight, and one of them coulda latched onto that bear."

I mumbled my thanks and walked away. The situation was hopeless. Aunt Queenie wouldn't go near those barrels in the basement in a million years.

When I broke the news to her and Tree, she said, "Homeless people go through other people's trash to survive. I suppose we can do it to find Joey's bear." I stared at her in disbelief as she handed Tree her car keys, saying, "It so happens, with the blood drive coming up, I have a box of rubber gloves in the trunk."

In the basement, as Tree dumped the contents of each barrel into an empty one, Aunt Queenie and I pawed through the falling debris. We found popcorn bags, Sno-Cone cups, cotton candy handles, and more—all of it covered with goo. But we didn't find Peanut.

When we peeled off our sticky gloves well after midnight, Tree's T-shirt was sweaty and streaked with rust from the barrels. Aunt Queenie's pencil was long gone from her topknot, her nail polish was chipped, and one of her nails was broken. Blotches of popcorn grease, red and purple Sno-Cone syrup, and pink cotton candy stained her lavender pantsuit.

I looked down at my own clothes. I was in the same shape as Aunt Queenie. Tears scalded my eyes. "It's my fault," I said. "I brought Joey to the circus, and I should have made sure he got home with Peanut."

"It's nobody's fault, Velveeta," said Tree. "It just happened."

"That's right," said Aunt Queenie. "He's always misplacing that bear. He could just as easily have lost it at the gym or church or somewhere."

All the way to Tree's house, they tried to make me see I wasn't to blame, but their words went in one ear and out the other.

At home, I showered, crawled into bed, and lay wide awake worrying about Joey. He'd been content in his own little world, until I came along and started changing things.

I needed to carve. Instead, I did the next best thing—I stained and painted the little wooden bear. When I was finished, he looked exactly like Peanut with that one black eye, the red neckerchief, the red plaid on the paws. I knew he could never take the place of the real Peanut, but at least Joey would have something to remember him by.

I set the carving on the nightstand, switched off the light, and lay sleepless again. The heat kicked on, and the warm-wax smell of Punky's crayons permeated the air.

I pictured Punky, spreading his wings at the sheltered workshop. After he died, I'd started spreading my wings, too, but it seemed as though I'd never soar gracefully. Oh, I flapped my wings and made the grand effort, but I always bumbled on the landings, like an albatross.

25

Excess Baggage

The alarm blasted me from a sound sleep. While shutting it off, I knocked Joey's bear to the floor. "What a klutz," I muttered, leaning out to pick up the carving. I turned on the radio, then buried my head under the blanket. I knew Joey would be incredibly sad this morning without Peanut. I figured he'd miss Special Olympics. Maybe Tree and Avanelle would go with me afterward to visit him. Maybe we could cheer him up.

A news reporter said, "A man who wandered away from Rest Haven Nursing Home was struck by a car last night at the intersection of Broadway and Peece. Authorities say the victim, twenty-three-year-old Joey Marcum, has the mind of a child. . . ."

Fear jolted me upward so fast, I got tangled in the covers.

". . . not seriously injured. However, because he has a history of heart problems, ambulance personnel rushed him

to a Jefferson City hospital, where he was treated and released. . . ."

I shot out of bed and raced to the kitchen.

"I heard," said Aunt Queenie, her face as white as her
Special Olympics sweatshirt.

"He was looking for Peanut," I said.

"You don't know that for sure."

My temper flared. "Yes, I do! It's my fault he almost got
killed walking the streets! You don't have to smooth things
over, make it easier for me, just because I'm your *responsibility!* If you've got to pamper somebody, pamper Joey, not
me!"

Aunt Queenie's face was red, her mouth a perfect "O."
Her hand fluttered to her cheek—a hand with chipped polish and a broken nail.

Suddenly, I saw her in that stained lavender pantsuit, and
I was ashamed of my outburst. "I'm sorry. I should bite my
tongue off."

Aunt Queenie turned away, then folded and unfolded the
cuffs of her sweatshirt. Finally, she looked back at me with
watery blue eyes. "Sometimes, Delrita, I just don't understand you."

I didn't understand me, either. How could I have been
so hateful? I wanted to tell her it was anger at myself, not
at her, that made me spout off like Old Faithful. I wanted
to put my arms around her, to feel her arms around me. But
I kept quiet and stayed put.

I wasn't sure why. Maybe because I was stubborn. Maybe
because she hadn't denied that I was a responsibility. Maybe
because this was Saturday.

Special Olympics.

In the deepest, darkest part of my soul, I resented the fact that everybody but me would be hugging the queen.

I pulled on jeans and my own Special Olympics sweatshirt, rammed my feet into sneakers, and ran a brush through my hair. Frowning at the bags under my eyes, I yanked the sweatshirt off. No way could I help with the basketball toss this morning. I had to check on Joey. The doctors might have missed something, or his heart might still act up. I had to see him for myself.

I donned the four-leaf-clover T-shirt, shoved Joey's bear into my jeans pocket, and hurried back to the kitchen. "I can't go to the gym," I said. "I've got to go see Joey."

"Well, I declare, Delrita," said Aunt Queenie, frowning at me through the steam from her coffee cup. "Why not just call his mother and ask how he is? We'll visit him together and take him flowers this afternoon. People are counting on you this morning."

"They'll just have to count me out. I've got to see Joey. Now." I pulled the bear from my pocket. "I finished this last night. I thought maybe it would help."

Aunt Queenie looked at the bear. "As a work of art, it's beautiful. As a peace offering, it probably won't do much good. Joey has lost something he held dear, and his mother could have lost her son. I doubt that either one of them will be appeased by a chunk of painted wood."

Our eyes locked, and Aunt Queenie stared me down. Her message was loud and clear: No smoothing things over this time.

After that, uncertainty plagued me like a gnat. I tried to prepare myself for what I would find at the nursing home. Joey with bumps and bruises and a bandage or two. His mother hovering over him, her loving expression changing to anger when she spotted me.

At Rest Haven, some residents were seated in the dining hall, while others were eating breakfast off trays in their rooms. The combined smells of coffee, eggs, oatmeal, and urine made my high-fiber cereal ricochet in my stomach.

I felt a huge tug on my heartstrings when I spied Joey lying face up on his bed, red spread pulled up to his chin and hands folded over his round belly. His mother's bed was empty . . . and so was Peanut's bamboo chair. I supposed Mrs. Marcum was in the dining hall and Joey wasn't hungry for breakfast.

Despite the lump in my throat, I managed an upbeat "Hi!" as I moved toward him.

He didn't respond. His good eye stayed fixed on the ceiling. His bad eye, ringed by a bruise, rolled like a useless marble.

I touched his hands. Ice cold. The right one was wrapped in gauze, the skin around the bandage red and puffy. He had a knot on his forehead and a deep, raw place on his cheek, as though he'd skidded face-first on pavement.

I glanced anxiously at his mother's bed. Hungry or not, how could she leave him at a time like this? "Joey, I can't tell you how sorry I am you got hurt." He looked at me and blinked, so I kept talking. "I'm sorry, too, about Peanut. Somebody must have picked him up at the circus, because we looked through tons of trash and couldn't find him."

Joey blinked again, and a tear rolled onto his pillow.

I swallowed hard, but I couldn't get rid of that lump. I pulled the bear from my pocket and eased it between his folded hands. "You made a magic picture for me, so I made this little critter for you."

Joey's gaze darted from the bear to Peanut's chair and back again. More tears rolled onto the pillow.

I knew then I'd made a mistake—no, a major blunder. Joey didn't need a reminder of Peanut. He needed the real thing.

I ran from the room. I couldn't fight my own tears any longer, and it wouldn't help Joey to see me bawling.

Head down to hide my crying, I walked up and down the hallways, trying to pull myself together so I could go back and sit with him. When my tears ran out, I was standing in the doorway of Sergeant Roebuck's room. I needed to talk to somebody, and he would fill the bill.

"Come on in, girlie," he said, pushing away his tray. "You're a lot easier to look at than oatmeal and prunes."

I clomped in and plopped onto the chair beside his bed. "Have you still got two ears?"

"And two good eyes. So tell me why you flapped in here like a bird with a broken wing."

I told him how I'd bumbled—with Aunt Queenie first, then Joey.

He rubbed his jaw, and his whiskers rasped like sandpaper on wood. "Sounds to me like excess baggage," he said.

"What?"

"You're carrying too much guilt. Queen does go overboard on the pampering. As for Joey, well, he'll bounce back in a day or so. He'll attach himself to something else, and he'll be back creating his magic the same as always. The Lord makes folks like him in a special way, and it don't take much to make them happy."

Two images fluttered across the screen of my mind—Peanut in his bamboo chair, and Mom's Bruno Bear in that old rocking chair. It was possible that Joey could love Mom's bear, if only I knew where it was.

"You know, girlie," Sergeant Roebuck said, "I think it would help if you'd talk more to Queen. Tell her how sad and mixed up you feel sometimes. It sure helped me to talk out my feelings about the war."

I nodded, just so he'd know I was listening.

"Like you said the other day, I've been torturing myself with the past. No more. I've finally made peace with myself." A smile creased his face, and he added, "You see, girlie, if I'd died at the hands of the Nazis, Queen wouldn't exist. She wouldn't be here to take care of you."

I was glad that revelation made him feel better, but it didn't help me. Aunt Queenie didn't want the job.

"Another thing," Sergeant Roebuck went on, "if I get this dad-blamed cast off my leg, I plan to attend that D-Day reunion. Those guys don't need to hear Leo's story, but I need to tell it, 'cause he died trying to take care of me. That's been *my* excess baggage. Reckon if the story's off my chest and the duffel bag's in the attic, I can clear the cobwebs from my brain."

Attic. Cobwebs. I sat stunned, staring at Sergeant Roebuck.

"What's the matter, girlie? You look like you swallowed a bug."

I leaped to my feet and kissed his bristly cheek. "Thanks, Mr.—Sergeant Roebuck. You just helped me solve my problem."

"I did? How? You mean you're gonna talk to Queen?"

"No. I'll explain later. Gotta go."

"Girlie, what—"

But I was flying out his door. I ran toward the entrance, certain that Mom's Bruno Bear was in the attic at our house. Not Uncle Bert and Aunt Queenie's house. *Our* house, where I'd lived with Mom and Dad and Punky.

I hit the crash bar on the outer door and burst into the sunlight before indecision struck me. My bounding steps slowed to a crawl. I hadn't even *seen* that house since the day after my parents died. Could I go back to it now? Could I knock on the door like a stranger? Could I walk through rooms where every piece of furniture, every picture on the wall was forever entrenched in my memory?

No, I couldn't do it. I'd have to send Uncle Bert. Then I recalled how he'd cried over those boxes in the garage. It wouldn't be any easier for him than it was for me. I trudged on.

You can do this, I told myself. You can do it for Joey.

26

A Little
Grain of Hope

My eyes stung as I made the journey to my home across town, visiting each room in my mind: The living room, where Punky's crayon wrappers and my wood shavings lay like litter in a hamster cage. The kitchen, where Mom fried chinny while Dad checked the newspaper for antique auctions. The bathroom, with Dad's shaving kit and Mom's hairbrush together by the sink. Their bedroom with the God's eye hanging from a knob on the highboy. Punky's bedroom with clowns from wall to wall. My room with the sea-green carpet, the room that was Heidi Grissom's now.

A little ways from the house, I stopped and blew my nose. Down the street, I caught sight of Marcus Gregory, playing cars in the gravel of his driveway. If I focused on him, I wouldn't see beyond the shrubs, wouldn't see my house as a whole. With my eyes riveted on his spiky blond hair, I moved on, remembering how he and Punky had played circus with clowns and animals in the dirt under the swing set. Marcus had been seven then; Punky, thirty-five.

"Delrita?" Marcus said, jumping up when he saw me. He'd grown taller, but the two cowlicks at his forehead still gave him a devilish look.

"Hi, Marcus," I said without slowing down. If I stopped to talk to him, I might never have the courage to pass those shrubs.

I could feel his eyes on me as I turned onto what used to be my sidewalk. My gaze never left the concrete.

As I neared the porch, a smothering sensation enveloped me. I gulped air, trying to suck in enough oxygen to get me up the steps.

One step, two steps, three. I stared at the door, at that nickel-sized hole made when Dad's lawnmower flung a rock.

My legs wobbled. I was bonkers for doing this. I should turn around and leave right now. But I lifted a hand and knocked on the spot beside the hole.

Maybe no one was home.

Footsteps.

Maybe the person would think I was nuts and slam the door in my face.

The knob was turning.

Run!

Too late. The door swung open, and a lady with chestnut hair and a wrinkled face peered at me over silver-rimmed spectacles. "Hello," she said.

I knew her from somewhere. Those wrinkles, like a shar-pei. I remembered then. I'd seen her reading poetry to Madeline Zang at the nursing home.

"I—uh—I'm Delrita Jensen," I stammered, "and I'm—uh—looking—"

"—for Heidi?" she finished, shaking her head. "She's not here. Could I help you with something? I'm her grandmother, Abigail Naramore."

"Well, actually, I'm not looking for Heidi. I—uh—used to live here."

"Oh, that's why your name rang a bell. Or maybe I heard it from Heidi. Doesn't matter. So tell me, if you didn't come to see Heidi, what brings you here?"

I stumbled through an explanation that sounded crazy, even to me.

But Mrs. Naramore must have thought I was harmless. She took my hand, drew me inside, and shut the door. "Goodness, hon. You're shaking like a leaf."

I stared at my feet. "I'll be all right. It's just—I—It was hard for me to come here."

"I can imagine. Please, sit down."

I dropped onto the nearest seat—an unpadded wooden bench. Whomp! My tailbone got rammed clear up to my ribs. When I recovered, I sat blinking at my surroundings. Scarred wooden desks, another old bench, wallpaper with ABC's and numbers. Obviously, the decor was old-time schoolhouse, but it was the ugliest living room I'd ever seen.

A bubble of hysteria rose in my throat. To disguise my snort of laughter, I ducked my head and pinched my nose.

"You poor child," Mrs. Naramore said. "Can I get you anything? A drink of water maybe?"

"No, thanks," I sniggered. "I'll be okay in a minute."

"I heard about that young man on the radio this morning," Mrs. Naramore said. "So he wandered away looking for his bear? Do you really think your mother's bear could be in our attic?"

I only nodded, because I still felt the urge to giggle my head off.

"Then let's have a look."

I followed her, aware now that her pedal pushers and short-sleeved shirt revealed age spots on her skinny limbs.

Ugh! Someone had painted the kitchen cabinets yellow and stenciled fruit on the doors. The curtains were yellow-and-white-checked, and so was the oilcloth on the table.

Mrs. Naramore fished a flashlight from a drawer, handed it to me, and headed for the door to the garage. "We're not very organized yet from the move," she said, "so you'll have to excuse the mess out here. So many cartons, there's hardly room for my car. I've been after Walter to store them in the attic, but he's been too busy learning about the antique shop. There's a stepladder. Since I'm not as spry as I used to be, you'll have to do the climbing."

The garage looked like a warehouse, not at all like Dad's workshop, and the air smelled of musty cardboard and engine oil, not freshly sawn lumber. After positioning the ladder under the attic entry, I climbed up and hauled myself through the hole.

I played the flashlight in a circle around me. Dust, cobwebs, boxes, a spittoon, my toy chest . . . and Mom's old rocking chair. A knot of sadness formed in my throat when I saw her handwriting on some of the boxes: "Christmas decorations" and "Stuff from the farm."

Gingerly, I peeled back the flaps on the first farm box. Baby clothes, probably mine. I held up a pink jumpsuit and grinned. Even then I'd had pipe-cleaner legs.

The knot in my throat eased. I sneezed twice and plowed into more boxes. Income tax papers, account records of soybeans and corn, workbooks I'd had in elementary school, miscellaneous shoes and work boots. In the fifth box, packed in with tablecloths and curtains, I found what I was looking for—Bruno Bear.

"Pay dirt," I said, tossing the bear to Mrs. Naramore before climbing down the ladder. At the bottom, I sneezed again.

"Come in and wash the dust off," she said. "I'll fix you something to drink."

"I've been too much trouble already."

"No trouble at all. Just make yourself at home while I get your drink."

Make myself at home. I rinsed off at the kitchen sink and dried on a paper towel, being careful not to glance out the window into the backyard where Punky's swing set had stood.

Mrs. Naramore handed me a glass of orange juice and pointed to the table. "Pull up a chair, hon."

I sat down, clutching Bruno on my lap. He smelled like the farmhouse, like wood smoke. I thought of Dad at the farm, coming in the back door after feeding the livestock, stamping snow off his boots, and warming his hands over the big black stove in the kitchen. I thought of the saying, "Home is where your loved ones are. It's where you hang your heart." Suddenly, in this awful yellow kitchen, I felt a blessed release. This house was just a house now. It was home to the Naramores and Heidi and had nothing to do with me.

"I don't know what else you found in the attic, but if you want it, it's yours," Mrs. Naramore said as she joined me at the table. "Walter can bring it to you one of these days."

"Thanks. I—uh—thanks." I stared at the checks on the tablecloth. Her kindness made me feel like pond scum for the way I'd treated Heidi.

"Are you in the eighth grade, too?"

I nodded.

She chuckled and gathered some crumbs into a pile with her finger. "Then I'll bet you've been talking to a combat veteran. Heidi's interviewing a prisoner of war."

"So that's where she is," I said, trying to pick up my end of the conversation.

"No. At the moment, she's visiting her mother."

"She's back from Europe?"

Mrs. Naramore's head shot up. "Europe? Madeline's never been to Europe."

I felt my eyebrows scrunch together. How could you shoot photographs in Europe if you didn't go there first?

Mrs. Naramore started crying, and I added two and two. Heidi had made up that story about her mother. But why?

Not a sound was coming from Mrs. Naramore, but her whole body was shaking and tears were sliding down her cheeks. I looked at Bruno, at the checkered curtains, at the fruit stencils on the cupboard doors—anything to keep from seeing her carry on like that.

After getting up to fetch a paper towel for her, I shifted from one foot to the other, wondering what to do. Should I leave? Should I stay? Should I call the antique shop and tell Walter, "Come home quick. Your wife's having a nervous breakdown"?

At last, her tears stopped rolling. She shuddered and mopped her face. "I'm sorry, hon. That's been coming on for a long time, but it's too bad you had to see it. If you'd care to sit down, I'll try to explain."

I sat down again with Bruno in my lap. It seemed a small miracle he was still intact. I'd been squeezing him hard enough to pop his stuffing out.

"Heidi's mother is in the nursing home," Mrs. Naramore said. "In a vegetative state."

I felt as though a balloon had inflated in my chest. In a flash of memory, I heard Mrs. Naramore reading poetry. I saw Heidi, pale as dough, carrying a treasury of nursery rhymes. Madeline Zang was Heidi's mother. Until this moment, I'd missed the connection, because when Mrs. Naramore answered the door, I was all upset about the house.

"Madeline was a photographer, and traveling Europe with her camera was her dream," Mrs. Naramore said, lacing and unlacing her fingers. "I had no idea Heidi was telling that story, and that's why it came as such a shock." She wiped a hand across her mouth before going on. "I'll spare you the details. Suffice it to say that Madeline was an alcoholic and the victim of . . . a terrible accident. That—that—person in the nursing home is not my daughter, nor Heidi's mother, but a shell. An empty shell."

I didn't know what to say. Anything I came up with would be woefully inadequate, like the endless phrases uttered to me after my parents died. Technically, Madeline Zang was alive. Machines were pumping air in and out of her body, but the love and the laughter were gone.

And yet, the family had seized onto a little grain of hope. Mrs. Naramore read poetry to Madeline, in hopes she'd make that long journey back. Heidi was probably reading nursery rhymes to her this very minute.

"Mrs. Naramore," I said, touching her hand. "That Europe story? Maybe Heidi tells it to keep her mother's dream alive."

27

Zero Hour

I left the house, wondering about Madeline Zang's terrible accident. Had she been driving drunk?

Marcus was still running cars in the gravel. Shading his eyes from the sunlight, he cast me a wary glance. "Was it hard going back there?"

"At first it was, till I got inside. It's nothing like home anymore."

He gazed mournfully toward the backyard. "There's nobody for me to play with now. I wish Punky hadn't died."

"Me, too." I tousled his hair and hurried past. Early on, Marcus had spied on Punky out of curiosity, and I'd labeled him "that bratty Gregory kid." How wrong I'd been.

With a sinking feeling, I realized that I'd been wrong, too, in getting rid of my parents' most prized antiques. I wanted Mom's rocking chair from the Naramores' attic. I wanted her china cabinet from the antique shop, and the highboy and the old seaman's chest where Dad had stored all his junk. Was it too late to buy them back?

I glanced at Bruno, riding close to my heart. I wanted to keep him forever, sitting in that rocking chair.

"Forget that," I whispered, and removed his left eye. The thread was so old that only a few twists on the button made it pop off in my hand. I dropped it into the pocket of my jeans.

Looking straight ahead, I let my thoughts circle around Heidi. Her mother's name was Zang, not Grissom. Had she divorced Heidi's father? Had she ever even married him? Was the man really on a secret mission, or was he a carpenter or a bookkeeper or a telephone lineman?

I finally decided it didn't matter. What mattered was that I'd been unfair to Heidi. I'd brushed off her efforts to be my friend. Part of the problem had been the house, but that was no excuse now. That left teenage rivalry—two girls liking the same boy.

Could I be friends with Heidi if she kept after Tree?

Maybe.

Wasn't I the girl he'd kissed on the forehead? Wasn't I Velveeta, the spicy kind with jalapeño peppers? Wasn't I his all-weather friend?

The door to Madeline Zang's room was closed, but I could hear Heidi reciting a rhyme about whippets and snippets and a bucket in Nantucket. When she finished, I tapped lightly on the door.

"Who is it?"

"Delrita Jensen."

Silence. Seconds later, Heidi opened the door just enough to slip through it, then drew it shut behind her and kept her hand on the knob. The bow in her hair matched the sparkly blue in her T-shirt and accented the blue of her eyes. "Hi," she said with a tentative smile as her gaze flickered from Bruno to my face.

"Hi. Um, Heidi, could we talk? In your—in the room?"

"Talk about what?"

"About you and me . . . and how sorry I am about your mom."

The color drained from her face as she fell back against the door. "You know?" she whispered.

"I know."

She twisted the knob, letting her weight on the door pull her into the room.

I followed her inside, where the hissing of the machines sounded like a teakettle about to sing. A coldness crept into my bones when I saw Madeline Zang, close up, with the treasury of nursery rhymes leaning against her pillow. She was still lying on her back, but today her eyes were open, unseeing. At the end of her chestnut braid was a blue bow that matched Heidi's. I realized that Heidi's painting in sepia tones was a picture of her mother.

Heidi motioned for me to take the chair, while she propped her backside against the windowsill.

I inched the chair around to face her, sat on it, adjusted my jeans at the knees, situated Bruno on my lap, and cleared my throat. I was stalling, and Heidi knew it. She was gripping the windowsill with both hands and staring holes through me. "You're—uh—probably wondering what I'm doing with this teddy bear," I said.

"No, I'm wondering how you found out about my mother."

"Your grandma told me."

She slumped against the window, and scuffed one sneak-ered foot back and forth on the carpet until someone went by whistling in the hall.

"I thought I'd be safe telling that story about Mother in Europe," she said. "In Arkansas, all the kids knew the truth, but when we moved here, I figured nobody would ever have to know. I mean, how many teenagers hang out in a nursing home?"

"Quite a few in Tangle Nook, since Teen Buddies got started."

"I know that now," said Heidi, her voice flat and life-less. "I didn't know it then." All at once, she straightened up, crossed her arms, and stared at me, her blue eyes smol-dering. "I just wanted to make a fresh start. I'm tired of feel-ing ashamed, of having kids laugh behind my back."

That threw me for a loop. What brand of kids would laugh about a crippling car accident?

"Mother was in a rehab center three times—once for each divorce. The last time, she swore to me she'd never buy another drink. Oh, she kept her promise not to *buy* liquor, but she bartered for it in the Ozark Mountains. Photographs for homemade whiskey. Moonshine. The moonshine poisoned her."

My mouth dropped open, and Heidi realized she'd said too much. "You didn't know that?" she croaked.

"No! Your grandma said 'accident,' so I thought she meant a car wreck!"

"I guess you would, considering what happened to your parents."

My thoughts were reeling. Moonshine. White lightning. Rotgut. Men in the Ozarks had been breaking the law to brew it—and drink it—for generations. It didn't make sense that it had poisoned Heidi's mother.

Heidi saw the question in my eyes. "It's lead poisoning," she said. "Lead from the old car radiators used as condensers in the stills. Steam deteriorates the solder and leaches out the lead. The sheriff said it could have leached out from any one of the stills, or all of them."

"The sheriff?"

"Yeah. He knows the stills are there, but they're hidden so well, he can't find them. Isn't that a kick? The sheriff can't find the stills, but Mother did. In a way, at least. She got the liquor."

"How?"

"Call it the mountain grapevine. When a woman saw her neighbor's photo, she'd want one of her family, too, and she'd send word to Mother. The deals were all hush-hush, under-the-table, because the women paid off in moonshine."

"Then how did you find out?"

"Mother had a logbook in her car." Heidi looked away from me then and scraped at the polish on her fingernails. I doubted that the kids in Arkansas had laughed at her situation. Most likely it was all in her head.

I was sure of it when she said defensively, "We didn't

know any of this until it was too late. We thought Mother had the flu and couldn't get over it, but we couldn't make her go to the doctor. She was vomiting, not eating, not acting like herself. She got real bad headaches and couldn't remember things. Then she went into convulsions . . . and a coma."

"Is she—is it permanent?"

"Maybe not, if they can flush the lead out of her system. But she might always have nerve damage."

I stroked Bruno absently and wondered, What kind of life will she have if she ever wakes up?

Heidi shifted her position, and a sunbeam lit the bow in her hair. I thought of her pinning the bow in her mother's hair, of reading nursery rhymes, of keeping the dream alive. I heard that hissing, like a teakettle about to sing.

"I suppose everybody in Tangle Nook'll know the story now," Heidi said in the dark tone of defeat.

"They won't hear it from me."

Her face perked up. "You're not gonna tell?"

"Nope. But you know what? I think you'd feel better if you told it yourself. Then you can stop worrying about getting caught. When Avanelle moved to Tangle Nook, she bent over backwards to keep it secret that her dad was in prison. Tree told the whole football team."

"Telephone, television, and tell-a-Tree," Heidi said.

So Tree had let her in on the joke. Jealousy pricked my heart, and I realized being friends with her was going to be harder than I thought.

"Delrita, all that stuff about my dad—I just want you to know it's sort of true."

Sort of true? Was that like sort of going to Europe? With Heidi, who was so flamboyant about everything, maybe the truth was always out in left field somewhere. I had a feeling that even if her father was a window washer, she'd have him polishing panes on the Empire State Building.

She said, "When Nana and Gramps found out Mother would need long-term care, they moved here so I could be close to Dad. He's in the OSI—Office of Special Investigations—at Whiteman Air Force Base. It's not exactly a secret mission, but he travels a lot and he can't talk about his work."

I stared at a cobweb stuck in the strings of my sneaker. Heidi's tale about her mother was understandable, but the one about her father was harder to accept. How easy it would be to blab the truth and tarnish Heidi's image.

And then, in my mind, I saw her as a turtle on a fence post, paddling thin air all by herself. This was the zero hour. I could lift her down, or I could leave her stuck on the post. I drew a deep breath and said, "Sounds like a secret mission to me."

"Delrita, I—Thanks."

I shrugged and stood up. Since I was in the turtle-helping business, I gave it one more shot. "Heidi, I've got lots of tools and basswood. Come over to my house tomorrow and we'll see what you can do."

"Do you mean it? You'll give me some pointers on carving?"

"You've got it," I said, then pointed my nose at the door and headed for it, before I could change my mind.

28

Lighter
Than Air

A cart loaded with lunch trays was clattering toward me. Moving back from the line of fire, I glanced at my watch. Almost noon. Three hours had passed since I'd left Joey's room.

Painfully conscious of Bruno's wood-smoke smell, I made my way down the hall. I expected to find Joey lying in bed, still pining away after Peanut. I expected his mother to throw daggers at me.

In the Marcums' doorway, I stopped short and did a double-take. Joey was on his bed, bouncing away on his rump! He was all dressed up in jeans and a red western shirt, his red neckerchief, and his red boots. Outrageous was trying to comb his blond curls, and Avanelle was trying to thread the Elvis belt through his pant loops.

"Careful, Tree. That bump on his forehead's bound to be tender."

That was Aunt Queenie's voice! When I peeked around

the door to my left and saw her, my jaw went slack. She looked like a much younger version of herself. Maybe it was the new brown teddy bear cradled in her arms. Maybe it was her outfit. The scarf holding her hair back matched her rose-colored sweater and slacks, and her face had only a touch of makeup.

"Hold still, Joey," she said. "The sooner you get ready, the sooner we can go."

I finally got my mouth to work. "Go where? What's going on?"

Everyone turned to look at me.

Joey waved his bandaged hand, saying, "Weeta! M-m-my mama!"

"Well, I declare," said Aunt Queenie. "Where in the world have you been?"

I sidled into the room. "Heidi Grissom's house."

"You went to Heidi's *house?*" asked Avanelle, shooting a bewildered glance at Tree.

"I figured out Mom's bear was in the attic. Hers—hers is exactly like Joey's." A wave of sorrow washed over me as I handed him the bear.

Joey gave Bruno the once-over, then shoved him back at me.

Did he sense my sadness, as Punky always had? Did he know I wanted that bear? "It's yours to keep," I said. "I know it's not Peanut, but it's a special bear. My mom loved it a lot when she was a little girl. It's the same color as yours, and it's all raggedy from being hugged."

Favoring his shiner, Joey blinked twice and shook his head.

Aunt Queenie walked over and gently touched his skid-marked cheek. "Joey, I can understand why you wouldn't like a new bear, but Delrita's giving you one that's already broken in. It's even a bit battered, like you."

Joey crossed his arms and lifted his chin. No deal.

"The bear needs a bandanna," said Avanelle, and we all looked at Tree.

He checked the pockets of his overalls, but came up empty-handed.

With a sigh, Aunt Queenie adjusted the rose-colored pencil behind her ear. "I'll get a handkerchief from Pop," she said. "Anything to get this show moving."

She left, and I fired a volley of questions at Tree and Avanelle: "What show's she talking about? Why are you in costume? Why is everybody here? Where's Joey's mother?"

"M-m-my mama," said Joey.

Tree and Avanelle grinned at each other—maddening, slow grins that made me want to scream.

"You start," said Avanelle to her brother.

"Nah. Ladies first."

"Come on, you guys! I'm dying here!"

"Do you want all the details, or the condensed version?" asked Avanelle.

"I don't care. Just tell me what's going on."

Again, Avanelle grinned at Tree. "We heard on the radio about Joey's accident, so when we got home from Special Olympics, Tree changed into Outrageous, and we came to visit him."

"I don't get it. Aunt Queenie and I were supposed to visit

Joey together and bring him flowers. So why did she come early with you guys and a new teddy bear?"

"We're here on our own," said Avanelle. "She came because she had a message on the answering machine about Joey's mother."

"M-m-my mama," said Joey, bouncing hard enough to squeak the springs of the bed.

I was more confused than ever. "What about his mama?"

"She's in the hospital in Jeff City," Tree said. "Got sick last night while we were at the circus."

"M-m-my mama," repeated Joey.

"Well, I declare." I felt lighter than air as the truth struck me. He'd been hit by the car while searching for his mother, not Peanut.

"You *declare?*" giggled Avanelle. "You sound like your Aunt Queenie."

"She's been beating the bushes for you," said Tree. "She's taking Joey to visit his mom, and she wants you to go, too."

"M-m-my mama."

"I hate hospitals," I said.

"I'm not fond of them myself," said Aunt Queenie as she bustled back into the room, "but you do what you have to do. Surely you want to be there when Joey is reunited with his mother." She tied her father's bandanna around Bruno's neck and asked Joey, "How's that?"

"Ya," he replied, accepting the bear as he slid off the bed.

"All right, then. Let's go."

But Joey couldn't be hurried. He sat Bruno in the bamboo chair, found his pocket protector in the drawer of his nightstand, and dumped out half of its Magic Markers.

"Joey Marcum, I declare," said Aunt Queenie. "I practically broke my neck getting here when I found out about your mother. I thought you'd be champing at the bit."

With his clumsy fingers, he nested the little carved bear into the protector before inserting it in his pocket. Painstakingly, he turned the bear face out. Then he lifted Bruno from the bamboo chair, smiled at the world at large, and said, "M-m-my mama."

Birdie was digging in the yard, near the shiny red pickup that was parked behind her parents' station wagon. Her head jerked up when Aunt Queenie hit the brakes hard enough to leave rubber on the street.

"That looks like Pop's truck," Aunt Queenie said.

But I pictured Sergeant Roebuck handing over the keys, and it looked like a turtle to me.

"It is his truck," said Tree as we stopped in front of the house. "He let Dad bring it over this morning. He wants him to drive it so the tires won't rot."

"Well, I declare."

Birdie came running as Tree and Avanelle got out of the car, and Aunt Queenie lowered her window to say hi.

"What happened to the bird nest on—" Birdie began, but Avanelle cut her off by clamping a hand across her mouth.

After a warning look at her sister, Avanelle dropped her hand and thanked Aunt Queenie for the ride.

"Don't go yet," called Mr. Shackleford, emerging from the house with Ellie in his arms. In the sunlight, his caterpillar eyebrows were almost black against the baby's orange curls.

"What happened to—" said Birdie, but Avanelle muzzled her again.

Tree chuckled as he tucked his fists under the bib of his overalls and watched his father's approach.

Mr. Shackleford, all smiles, stopped beside the car. "Somebody up there likes this family," he said. "I've got a job, I've got wheels, and I just heard the twelve o'clock newscast. The police have arrested two men for those burglaries. Seems one of them beat up his girlfriend, and she called the police and turned him in. They found stolen merchandise in the house. To save his hide, the fellow squealed on the other guy." He paused to wiggle his eyebrows at Avanelle. "It wasn't me, and it wasn't Slim."

"Yah-hoooo!" yelled Tree. He yanked open the car door, pulled me out, and whirled me around and around.

The next thing I knew, we were sprawled on the ground and the world was spinning crazily.

"Sorry about that. I stepped in a hole," said Tree, catching my hands to help me up. "Are you hurt?"

"No," I giggled. "Just a little dizzy."

"It was the only way I could think of to get you by yourself."

I noticed then that we were in the side yard, out of sight of Aunt Queenie's car. "Wh-what?"

Tree's gaze locked with mine. "I wanted to be alone for a minute with my all-weather friend," he said, his eyes like smoky green glass. "I know how hard it was for you to go back to your old house, but you did it to get Joey that bear."

"He didn't need it," I breathed, focusing on his blacked-out teeth. "He needed his mama."

"But you didn't know that."

"No, I—"

"What time is it?" Tree lifted my hand and glanced at my watch. "Twelve-nineteen. Then I've been wanting to do this for nineteen minutes."

"Do what?"

"This," he said, and kissed me squarely on the mouth.

It was unexpected. It was awkward. It was fast. I told myself his aim was bad, that he'd meant to kiss my forehead. "I—I—guess I reminded you of Birdie?"

"Guess again," he said.

Could he hear my heart hammering like a loose board in a hurricane? The storm of blood cells rushing to my face? I smiled into his emerald eyes and read the long-range forecast. Blue skies, fluffy clouds, mostly sunny weather.

29

A Walking Paradox

Forty minutes and at least that many "my mama's" later, we reached the hospital. Daydreaming about Tree had been a lifesaver for me, but Aunt Queenie was a bundle of nerves.

"I declare," she sighed as she helped Joey from the car. "I'm so tired of hearing *that phrase,* it's a miracle I haven't pulled my hair out."

"M-m-my mama," he said.

I might have laughed, except that seeing the hospital, knowing I had to go inside, had filled me with a sudden dread.

We rode the elevator to the third floor, and walked through a vast, endless hallway, our footsteps clicking against the tile and my pulse pounding in my ears. The smell of medicines and disinfectant. White uniforms everywhere. That nasal voice on the intercom, paging one doctor after another. All were painful reminders that no one had been able to save Punky.

"M-m-my mama," Joey announced to the people we met.

Some gawked, some grinned, some said "hello"—but no one ignored the chubby cowboy in red with the banged-up face, the raggedy teddy bear, and one leg shorter than the other.

We found Mrs. Marcum sleeping on her side with her twisted hands folded beneath her chin.

Joey cried, "M-m-my mama!" and hurled himself against her bed.

She yelped at the rude awakening, but she opened her arms when she saw him. "Here, son. Give me a hug."

"Ya!" He dropped Bruno at his feet and hugged her hard.

I felt a stinging in my throat. Joey would be happy anywhere, as long as he had his mama. I stared at Bruno. I was itching to snatch him back, to keep that little part of my mother.

"Mrs. Marcum," said Aunt Queenie, "how are you?"

"Better now that I can see Joey's okay."

"M-m-my mama," he said.

Mrs. Marcum patted his hand. "Son, I'm going to be fine. It was just a reaction to some new medicine, and I'll be out of here in a day or two. . . . What's that in your pocket?"

Joey handed her the carving, then picked Bruno off the floor and danced him across the covers.

"Where's Peanut?" his mother asked.

Aunt Queenie told her we'd lost him at the circus and that I was giving up Mom's bear.

Mrs. Marcum raised her eyebrows at me. "Are you sure you want to do that?"

"I'm sure. If Mom was here, she'd give it to him herself." The words made my throat sting worse. I mumbled something about needing a drink and escaped from the room. When I spied a STAIRWAY sign, I jogged down two flights of stairs and headed for the exit.

Outside, sitting on a bench, I watched a robin stretch a worm, and I watched the cars go by.

Nervously, I toyed with Bruno's eye button in my pocket. It made me think of Mom again, of giving up her bear.

I wished I'd stayed at home. If I had, I could be carving now and in control. I checked my watch. How long did Aunt Queenie plan to stay? Could I talk her into leaving now? Could we reach the antique shop before it closed?

I hurried back to Mrs. Marcum's room. No Aunt Queenie. Just Mrs. Marcum dozing with Bruno under her arm, and Joey making magic with his markers.

With a sense of urgency, I swept through the hospital's corridors, and when I didn't find Aunt Queenie, I made the trip again. This time, I checked more thoroughly, even glancing through the windows of some swinging doors marked MATERNITY WARD.

That's where I spotted her, halfway down a long hallway, standing motionless, entranced. What was she looking at? Newborn babies? I moved closer to the door. Yes, tilted up in a display window were three bassinets holding three small bundles—two blue, one pink.

I backed up and read the sign: MATERNITY WARD VISITING HOURS 1 TO 3 P.M. AND 7 TO 8:30 P.M., FAMILY MEMBERS ONLY.

Incredible! Aunt Queenie had broken the rules.

Slowly, dreamily, she reached out and touched one hand to the glass that separated her from the bundles. She stood that way for a long time, and I stood watching her, expecting any minute that an irate nurse would come charging out, commanding her to leave.

No nurse came, so I opened one swinging door and slipped inside. This hallway was carpeted, and one of my sneakers squeaked on the aluminum strip that separated carpet from tile. Aunt Queenie turned at the sound. Her face brightened, and she motioned for me to come for a closer look at the babies.

When I reached her side, the pink bundle squirmed and the tiny, wrinkled girl started squalling. The sound, muffled by the glass, was that of a kitten mewling.

"Wish I could pick her up and cuddle her," said Aunt Queenie wistfully. "I've always wanted a baby girl, but it wasn't meant to be. Sometimes my arms just feel so empty."

I remembered her cuddling that brand-new teddy bear. Had she pretended it was a real, live baby?

Aunt Queenie stood up straighter and retied the scarf in her hair. "I'm being silly, Delrita, because I have a child to love. You're not little anymore, but you very much need a mother, and that job fell to me. I know I can never take Shirley's place, but still, you're like a daughter to me. I keep hoping someday we'll be close, like a real mother and daughter ought to be."

I stopped breathing. Aunt Queenie *wanted* to be a mother to me?

"So far, I've had a hard time reaching you," she said, lifting my chin and staring into my eyes. "Don't you know you've added a new dimension to my life? That you've made my home complete? Someday, you'll fly off on your own, but for this little while, I want to keep you under my wings."

"But I—I thought I was just a responsibility."

Aunt Queenie's eyebrows shot upward. "Of course, you're a responsibility. That's what parenting is all about—responsibility tempered with love."

For a moment, I stood there, unmoving, letting it sink in that I wasn't just someone for Aunt Queenie to take good care of, or die trying. I fingered the button in my pocket, and let the memory of an army button flit across my mind. Leo had died trying to take care of Orvis Roebuck. The sergeant's voice rang in my ears: "For Leo, the war ended back in that little village. I was helpless and dying, and he saved my life. I was the turtle he set off the post."

In a flash of insight, I saw Aunt Queenie helping others, finding every turtle that needed rescuing and lifting it off its post.

And I was the prime turtle.

She'd helped me in many ways after my parents died: Changing my room so it would feel more like home. Insisting I carve out in the open, so I couldn't hide in my shell. Boxing up Dad's scrapbooks and Mom's doilies for the day when I could deal with them. Talking Mrs. Marcum into letting me take Joey places, because she knew how much I missed Punky. Helping me search for Joey's bear.

Would I ever forget my prissy Aunt Queenie digging through the trash in her lavender pantsuit? No. No more than I could forget those boxes of keepsakes in the garage, stacked on the woodpile for a cold fireplace.

Aunt Queenie, I thought, you're a walking paradox.

The next thing I knew, she was a watery, wavering image, and I was sobbing and throwing my arms around her.

"Delrita! I declare!" she said, but the shakiness in her voice told me she was crying, too. When she clutched me tightly against her breast, I felt absolutely giddy to be hugging the queen.

"Delrita," she murmured, stroking my hair, "I've waited so long for you to stop holding back."

Holding back. That was the plain, unvarnished truth, and hearing her say it made me tingle with shame. I'd kept her at a distance all this time, because I'd wanted my parents, my home, my life the way it used to be. That's why I hadn't found a place to hang my heart. "Aunt Queenie," I snuffled, "I—I—"

"Ladies! Please!" The sharp voice came from a stout nurse who must have had nails for lunch. "This is a maternity ward, not a soap opera," she snapped. "Have your sob session someplace else."

Wiping away tears with her fingers, Aunt Queenie struck a regal pose and looked down her nose at the nurse. "I know this is a maternity ward. I detest soap operas. And this is hardly a sob sess—"

The woman grabbed us by the arms and hauled us toward the swinging doors.

"How dare you do this!" shrieked Aunt Queenie. "Release that child!"

Just shy of the doors, the nurse let go of us, but Aunt Queenie and I couldn't stop the momentum. We shot through like two battering rams.

Heads swiveled in our direction, and then all motion stopped. At least half a dozen people were gaping at us, but Aunt Queenie's feathers were ruffled now. She stalked back to the nurse and spoke through the glass in a voice that would blister paint: "Loosen up! You're worse than a dad-blamed, old-maid schoolmarm with her underwear in a twist!"

I burst out laughing, but Aunt Queenie's face was set in stone. "Come, Delrita," she said, sailing gracefully past me and down the hall.

I didn't move. I just kept laughing and staring at her dignified back until she turned a corner. She'd borrowed her father's expression, just as he'd borrowed hers. Next thing you know, she'd be chewing tobacco and spitting in a can. The more I thought about the situation, the funnier it got. I visualized the nurse chomping nails, her underwear in a twist. Finally, holding my sides, fighting hysteria, I trailed after Aunt Queenie.

When I rounded the corner, there she stood, arms crossed, waiting for me. "I declare, Delrita. Can't you be a bit quieter? This is a hospital, you know."

"Yeah," I cackled. "I know."

"I don't understand why you're laughing."

"That nurse. The way she looked at you. Like you were a royal pain."

Aunt Queenie adjusted the pencil behind her ear. Then, eyes twinkling, she leaned toward me and confided, "I can be. Queen Esther Holloway gets upset when someone lays a hand on you."

We linked arms and walked together down the hallway. I barely noticed the white uniforms, the nasal voice on the intercom, the antiseptic smell. The sensation was that of open air, and I was flying free.